POISONED

CARMEN DM GRAY

Poisoned
Copyright © 2021 by Carmen DM Gray

All rights reserved. No part of this publication may be reproduced, distributed, or transmitted in any form or by any means, including photocopying, recording, or other electronic or mechanical methods, without the prior written permission of the author, except in the case of brief quotations embodied in critical reviews and certain other non-commercial uses permitted by copyright law.

Tellwell Talent
www.tellwell.ca

ISBN
978-0-2288-5805-8 (Hardcover)
978-0-2288-5084-7 (Paperback)
978-0-2288-5085-4 (eBook)

Dedicated to

my husband, Morgan, and my beautiful
daughters, Annabelle and Willa.
Thank you for believing in me.

CHAPTER

Friday, June 11

"Wake up, sweetheart," I heard my yia yia call softly from the other side of my bedroom door.

"OK," I called back sleepily.

My grandmother had done that every morning since I arrived here two weeks ago. I rolled over and gave my cat, Shade, a scratch between her ears as she got to her feet and stretched. She nudged my face signalling me. "I know, you're ready to eat. Me too."

I threw on my satin housecoat and slippers. It was a warm summer morning but Yia Yia had kept her air conditioner on all night. It made the whole second floor of her farmhouse feel like a freezer. As Shade and I walked down the stairs, I scanned the banister wall littered with pictures of my mother, my yia yia and her friends, me when I was younger and a few pictures of the Greek islands where Yia Yia used to live. My favourite picture was of me and my best friend, Chloe. She was my "summertime friend" and Yia Yia's neighbour. Then last summer I came to visit and Yia Yia told me she had moved away. I never heard from her again. It was odd that she never tried to contact me after that. We had been such good friends. It didn't seem possible that she just left without a word. I always found that a little suspicious. I touched the picture wishing I could see her again.

Yia Yia had moved to Athenera from Greece after she adopted Sharron, my mother. Yia Yia had lived in Greece before then but never told me why she had moved so far away. Athenera had so much Greek culture and quite a few people spoke Greek as a first language. Luckily, they had classes in both Greek and English at the high school.

Shade darted down the stairs before me and as I neared the kitchen I slammed into a wall of delicious, familiar Greek cooking smells. It was the normal spread of courgette balls or *kolokithokeftedes*, *kagianas*, yogurt with honey and walnuts and baklava. Yia Yia was a fan of sweet treats in the morning. I loved mealtimes here. There was always fresh coffee brewing and the smell of it always made me feel warm and cozy.

Shade was frantically scratching at the door, so I let her out as quickly as possible and filled her food bowl.

"Good morning, Ivy, dear," Yia Yia sang.

"Good morning," I replied, bending down to kiss her forehead. I helped set the rest of the table. As I sat down, Yia Yia started talking about her plans for the day. Every day she had a different volunteering job or fundraiser. Her week went like this:

Monday: Humane society cleaning crew

Tuesday: Foodbank stock person

Wednesday & Thursday: Help out in the hospital NICU. She used to be a nurse and doula.

Friday: Help out at the library doing various odd jobs.

On the weekends it changed too much to keep track of, but this week she happened to be at the food bank again.

"Do you have anything planned, dear?" she asked, jotting down her list and passing it to me to read.

"Nothing exciting," I said, mixing more honey into my yogurt. "Probably just finish unpacking the last little bit. By the way, I want to put up some pictures in my room. Do you have a hammer and nails?"

"They are in the shed. But be careful."

After I helped clean up from breakfast, I let Shade in and trotted upstairs to unpack my books and pictures. I had been procrastinating unpacking. Even though I knew I was going to live with Yia Yia until I went to college at least, I was unfamiliar with staying put anywhere. I didn't want to get comfortable then have to leave again. Shade made herself cozy on my bed to watch me.

I threw open my curtains and cracked open the window next to my bed to let in a little fresh air. Sunlight flooded the room with a white glow, and Shade moved to bask in the strip of pure sunlight, her black fur attracting the heat. She'd soon be too hot and go lie in my sink to cool off.

I was glad to have an ensuite attached to my room so I didn't have to worry about hogging the bathroom with my morning makeup routine or the relaxing baths I took every so often.

I threw all my books on the shelf in the corner and put all my Greek mythology ones on my bedside table shelf. I loved to read before bed and had read these mythology books a hundred times over. My favourites were all the love stories between the gods or goddesses and mortals or other mythological beings. I found them fascinating. They never seemed to get stale no matter how many times I read them. Most of the stories didn't have happy endings and many of them involved incest and revenge killing. But I found it exciting to see how far some would go for love.

I set my laptop on my desk between my bookshelf and the door and turned on some music. Then I rummaged through the boxes to find all the framed pictures I wanted to hang. There were a few of my mother and me when I was young, but most of them were of my "friends." I really only had friends at my last school because we had actually lived there long enough for me to make some. I lost touch with a lot of them after I moved, but I still had them on social media.

Satisfied with my picture selection, I walked outside to the shed which backed onto the woods at the far edge of the property. I was armed with a can of spider killer and a rolled-up newspaper. I HATED spiders.

I couldn't help but look toward Chloe's old house next door. The roof over her bedroom had caved in a little. The last storm had really done a number on it. It looked like it had been abandoned for several years instead of just one. I wondered if Chloe or her family had left anything behind. I decided once Yia Yia was in bed I was going to go look. She would forbid me to go anywhere that dangerous, but now that I was here again, I had to know.

Otherwise, it would eat at me constantly and drive me insane. I was hoping Chloe had left something behind that would remind me of her or at the very least give me a clue as to where she had gone.

Chloe and I were both really into Greek mythology. While I was always intrigued by Persephone's tragic life, Chloe preferred the ruthlessness of Athena. One summer we even wrote our own myths and exchanged them with each other when we were done. I still had Chloe's tucked away in the back of my journal. I hoped she had made some new friends wherever she was now who liked that kind of stuff.

I opened the shed carefully and amazingly there were no bugs at all. Yia Yia was a crazy cleaner but did she really clean in here too? I pulled the string for the light and searched for the toolbox she had mentioned. Under a few rakes and shovels, I found an old, rusted tackle box. "This must be it," I thought opening it.

The lid squeaked open and instead of tools, there were a bunch of old photos. Some were in black and white, some in colour but they were all severely faded. As I sifted through them, I noticed the black-and-white ones were of people I didn't know and none of them were smiling. Then I found a few of my yia yia as a young woman with my pappous at various places in Greece, as well as their wedding. I kept shuffling until I found pictures of Sharron as a teenager and in her college years. She was so beautiful and seemed so happy, which I hadn't witnessed much growing up.

My relationship with Sharron was very strained. We hardly talked and I felt so disconnected I started calling her by her given name instead of Mom. She moved us around a lot when I was younger and even more so as I got older. I had never really had any friends and I was an only child, so I had no one to talk to. I had wished desperately for a brother or sister. She had more boyfriends than I could count, and we only saw Yia Yia in the summer, so I never really had anyone but Sharron to look up to.

I hated Sharron for taking me away from any of the friends I was trying to make in whatever town we temporarily settled in. We never stayed more than a year anywhere. I was sick of starting over; that's why I moved in with my yia yia. Sharron was moving to Lithuania (god only knows why), but I wanted to finish high school in one place and stick with it. My yia yia tried to explain away her daughter's incessant need to move around, but I still thought it was quite selfish to drag me all over, especially if I was happy where we were.

I came upon a weathered photo with burnt edges. It was of Sharron when she was probably about twenty-four or twenty-five years old. She was standing on a balcony that overlooked the ocean with a man I didn't recognize. At first glance, it looked like a couple in love on their honeymoon or something. They had their arms around each other, and Sharron was staring dreamily at the camera with her head against his chest. The man was looking down at her. His features were sharp and defined; he looked muscular and strong. I could only see his profile, but it sent a shiver through my very core. He wasn't smiling and something in his stance, demeanour and eye made me feel uneasy, like he was probably a very cruel, unfeeling man. Then I noticed my mom's belly. She was pregnant. . . With me!?

CHAPTER

2

This man had to be my father! It had to have been me. As far as I knew she had never been pregnant before. How could she have not told me about my father? I had asked many times, but she always said she was unsure who he was. In this picture, she had to be at least six or seven months along. This man had to be him. I had to ask Yia Yia about this.

I put all the photos back in the tackle box except the one of Sharron and my supposed father. I stuffed that one in my pocket and shut the tackle box. In my hurry, I slammed it down on my pinkie. I yanked it out and examined it. I guess I hadn't slammed it as hard as I thought because I wasn't feeling any pain. I put the tackle box back where I had discovered it, found the hammer and a box of nails and closed the shed.

Walking back toward the house, my head was a whirl of questions. Sharron lied, which wasn't surprising, but what would have been the harm in telling me his name? Did Yia Yia know? Why did he leave us? Did I ever even meet him? Out of the corner of my eye, I saw something black dart through the trees. I stopped short and stood very still. Thinking it was a bear or something that could probably eat me, I slowly scanned the edge of the woods along the property line. Not seeing anything, I sprinted to the house and upstairs to my room.

Yia Yia had left to get groceries and as I finished hanging the last picture, I heard her come into the entryway. I walked downstairs to help her bring them in but found she was already in the kitchen with some of the groceries. The rest were in the arms of an extremely cute guy.

"Oh, Ivy, this is Lucas. I ran into him at the market and he followed me here to help bring in the groceries even though I told him I had you to help," she teased.

"I don't mind. I never mind helping you, Mrs. Mavros," Lucas smiled playfully.

"Oh, you're such a sweet boy and a terrible flirt," Yia Yia joked.

Lucas blushed. He was tall, muscular with light-brown tanned skin, blue eyes and golden-blond curly hair that looked messy but like he almost styled it that way. A large sun was tattooed on his shoulder. I was so lost in examining his surfer's body that I didn't realize they were both looking at me expecting me to at least say hello.

"Hey, oh, hello, Lucas, nice to meet you," I said nodding.

Yia Yia smiled and left to hang up her keys and purse in the entryway.

"*Eímai timí na se gnoríso, to megaleío sas,*" he said, setting the rest of the shopping bags down on the table.

"Oh, I'm sorry, Lucas, dear," Yia Yia said as she re-entered the room, "but we haven't been keeping up with Ivy's Greek language lessons. She probably has no idea what you said." She looked embarrassed, but it wasn't her fault I had fallen behind. Sharron and I had moved around so much that it was hard to keep track of us, and Yia Yia wasn't always able to get a hold of me to teach me more of her native tongue.

Lucas wiped his hands on his shorts and offered one to me.

"I said, 'Nice to you meet you too.' " He smiled.

His hand was surprisingly warm and soft. He probably spent most of his time outside in the summer. I did know a few simple phrases, and I was rusty, but I was almost certain that what he said didn't mean, "Nice to meet you."

"Ivy, I bought you a few things for a quick breakfast," Yia Yia said, putting a tin of muffins on the table to show me. "I work almost every day this week and may not have time to cook too much."

I was still shaking Lucas's hand, and I wasn't helping her put anything away. I was lost in his gaze and touch.

"Ivy? Are you all right?" Lucas said. "You're sweating."

"Oh no," I thought. I was sweating. "Um . . . yeah, I'm OK." I let go of Lucas's hand and started helping Yia Yia put the groceries away. Shade was circling Lucas's legs, rubbing the sides of her body against him.

"Hi, kitty," Lucas said. In my mind, it was always a good sign when Shade liked someone. "Ivy, I'll see you Monday at school?" Lucas asked heading toward the front door.

My mouth was dry and with the risk of saying something stupid I just nodded.

"OK. Bye, Mrs. Mavros," he called over his shoulder.

"*Kalós agapitós*," Yia Yia called from the fridge. She would switch between English and Greek whenever she was around people who understood Greek. Which I did not. But I knew what she said loosely translated as "goodbye."

"Cute, isn't he?" Yia Yia winked. I blushed and tried not to grin, but I failed, and she saw. "Oh, it's OK, Ivy. He's impossible not to stare at. I may be old but I'm not dead." She laughed.

"Yia Yia, I'd rather not talk about boys with you." I giggled.

"Well, I'm all you've got for now."

After supper that night, I went back to my room with Shade running ahead of me. I found myself searching through my closet to find an outfit for the next day. I decided to go into town and go shopping for some things to wear to school. Everything I had was either too small or unflattering. Sharron never let me go shopping alone so most of what I had she had to approve of first … and she had the style of a nun. I had to beg Yia Yia to let me go alone, and I promised to be careful. You know . . . keep my cell phone on and charged and all that junk.

I settled on jeans and a simple black t-shirt. I was just going into town, so I didn't really care too much what I was wearing. I looked in the full-length mirror. I didn't feel I was very pretty, but my yia yia constantly told me I was beautiful. She must have been seeing something I wasn't. I was average height, slim but somewhat lanky and thin-faced, my hair was kind of dark chocolate brown but unruly and way too thick, my eyes were deep green, and my skin was perma-tanned. At least I had that going for me. While I was judging myself, I saw something at my window behind me. It startled me because I was on the second storey, and what I thought I glimpsed was a woman's face. Frightened, I turned around and slowly walked toward my window. Whoever it was darted into the forest. She must have been what I had seen in the forest earlier. I thought again about my plan to go to Chloe's house that night and decided it wasn't a good idea. I shut the window, locked it and closed my curtains. I considered telling Yia Yia what I had seen, but I didn't want to worry her.

I decided to sleep with my light on.

CHAPTER

3

Saturday, June 12

The next morning, I woke up to the usual exchange with Yia Yia except it ended with Yia Yia saying, "I'm volunteering at the food bank today, so I'll be there all day if you need me. Be careful. I love you."

As I was getting dressed, I heard her leave. She worked all over and always volunteered on the weekends if she didn't have something else planned. She was a remarkably busy lady.

I was excited to go into town; I went through my usual morning makeup routine: purple eye shadow to compliment my best feature (my eyes), black eyeliner and mascara (man I wish my eyelashes were longer) and light bronzer. I threw on the outfit I had picked the night before and grabbed an empty backpack before pulling my old bike out of the garage and riding into town. It wasn't far and despite the early hour, it was quite hot out.

Yia Yia's house was on a hilltop and the town was in a valley so it was downhill all the way. As the wind whipped my hair back, I breathed in the muggy air. The unexplained photo of my probable father was in my back pocket. The night before I had woken up constantly feeling a toxic need to look at it and every time I did it would fill me with dread. I couldn't seem to settle my mind. I had always wanted a father but something about him wasn't right. If he was my father, I hoped I'd never meet him.

I locked my bike to the rack beside a fountain in the middle of town. The little courtyard was surrounded by bakeries, cafés, organic fruit vendors and overpriced scent shops. It reminded me of Belle's village in *Beauty and the Beast*. Behind the Bean (my favourite coffee shop) was a thrift store called Helios. I had never been there before, but they had a sale going on, so I decided it was as good a place as any to find a few things for school. I wasn't much for buying brand-name clothes. If I thought something was cute, I bought it regardless of who the "designer" was. I wanted to look nice but also be comfortable. I sorted through the sale rack and as I was walking to the dressing room to try a few shirts on, I noticed someone watching me.

She was tall with blue eyes, short brown hair cut into a trendy bob and had golden tanned skin and a simple crescent moon tattooed on her right shoulder. She almost looked like a female version of Lucas. She dressed like him in that sort of surfer/workout attire: black leggings, a blue sheer workout top that showed off her black sports bra and spotless white running shoes.

I tried to ignore the stare, but I still felt her eyes on me as I made my way back from the dressing rooms. I picked through a few more clothes trying to shake the feeling of the weird girl and then felt a tap on my shoulder. I spun around and there she was with Lucas.

"Hey, Ivy," Lucas said, smiling.

"Hey." I smiled back. I looked beside him at the girl; she had a serious expression on her face. I couldn't tell if it was fear or hatred, but it looked kind of like both.

"Oh, this is Luna. My twin sister," he said noticing I was looking at her.

"Well, that explains it," I thought. "Nice to meet you, Luna," I said extending my hand to her. She looked at it and sneered.

"*Ta léme sto spíti, Lucas*," she said in a low tone, not taking her eyes off me. She turned around with such force that it sent a shock through me. I felt like I had to steady myself; she then briskly walked away from us.

I turned to Lucas who seemed tense. "Did I do something wrong?" I asked. I had only just met her. She didn't even know me but already seemed to dislike me.

"No, she's just not that friendly. . . . She likes to be alone." He shrugged.

"Oh, well I'm just shopping for school. What are you doing here?" I said, changing the unpleasant subject.

"Same, and I found a few things, but I was just about to get lunch. Would you like to join me? My treat," he said, trying to sweeten the deal before I even said anything. How could I say no?

"Sure, just let me pay for these clothes," I said, making my way to the register.

As we walked to the restaurant, the Peryton Café, I tried to keep the conversation light and not too personal until the infamous picture of my "maybe" father fell out of my back pocket.

"You dropped this," he said picking it up and handing it to me. I caught a glimpse of "its" face while folding it back up and automatically shuttered. I was lost in thought the rest of the way to the café and hardly said anything.

Once we were seated, Lucas broke the silence. "Is something wrong?" he asked, concerned.

"Just this picture. I'm not sure who the man in it is but . . . I think he might be my father that I've never met. Sharron, my mother, was always moving us around. We never really stayed anywhere for more than a few months and my mom always picked really unsafe places to live in."

"What do you mean? Like unsafe neighbourhoods?" Lucas asked.

"No, like cheap apartments with faulty wiring, cracked water pipes, little to no heat, no windows."

"Oh. That sounds horrible. I know how it feels to have an estranged father. I hardly ever see mine. It's just me and Luna. My father supports us from overseas."

I knew how he felt but I didn't want to say that. It never seemed genuine when someone said it.

"That must be hard for you and your sister," I said sympathetically.

He nodded.

"I always wanted to have a father growing up," I said. "It would have been great to have had a stable family. Maybe we wouldn't have moved around so much. But this guy, I hope I never meet him." I handed Lucas the folded picture. "I found it in Yia Yia's shed. Chloe and I used to play in there all the time, but I'd never noticed the tackle box full of pictures until yesterday."

"Chloe? You mean Chloe Ladas?" Lucas asked straightening up.

"Yeah, she was a good friend of mine. We hung out every summer; she lived right beside Yia Yia until her family moved away, and I never heard from her again."

"I knew her too. Not very well, but I remember her," he said sadly. We both shifted uncomfortably. It was weird talking about Chloe when neither of us had heard from her since she moved.

In an effort to change the subject to something a little less awkward I decided to get back to the picture dilemma. I needed someone else's opinion of this mystery man, and I didn't want to ask Yia Yia because there was undoubtedly bad blood there.

"Anyway," I offered, breaking the silence, "if you could look at the picture and tell me what you think . . .?"

He unfolded it and immediately dropped it, looking disturbed by what he saw. It was almost as if he saw something in the photo he was deathly afraid of. All the colour drained from his face.

"What's wrong?" I asked, picking up the picture again. Lucas was gripping the table hard, his knuckles bright white. "You barely looked at it."

Lucas's face was twisted in a look of disbelief and fear. "I'm sorry," he said, taking a deep breath. The colour slowly returned to his face and he seemed to regain his composure. "I thought I saw ... someone else. The man in that picture is terrifying though."

I looked at it again. I wouldn't say terrifying, but it seemed Lucas also believed there was something off about him. It was obvious Lucas was uncomfortable, so I changed the subject once again. "So, what do you recommend off the menu . . .?"

Silence . . . he seemed lost in thought as he stared at nothing in particular. This was even more awkward than the previous conversation. Thank god the waitress arrived just then. I ordered chicken souvlaki and he ordered spanakopita pie.

"So, what are you into? Are you interested in joining any school groups or teams?" Lucas asked as we ate.

"An extracurricular would be a great way to make friends," I thought. "I'm into art. Is there an art group?"

"As a matter of fact, there is. I'll introduce you to Ms. MacDonald on Monday. She's the art teacher and runs the after-school art projects," he said thoughtfully.

After we finished, we walked back to the thrift store. It was almost four o'clock! We had talked for nearly three hours! "I'm sorry," I said, "but I have to go. I told Yia Yia I would be home for supper."

"No problem, but let me drive you," he offered. "It's getting hotter and it'd be a lot easier than going up the hill on a bike."

I agreed with that, so we threw my bike in the back of his truck. I hopped in the front seat and noticed a sun-shaped air freshener hanging from his review mirror. The leather seats were cool to the touch and felt nice on this sticky day.

It was a short drive and with the gentle sound of the radio, I felt comfortable even though we didn't talk the whole time. "Thanks for the ride and lunch," I said as he helped me pull my bike from the truck box.

"If you don't have a way of getting to school, I can pick you up," he said hopefully.

I smiled. "Sure, that would be great. Give me your phone and I'll put my number in."

"OK, I'll text you later," he said taking his phone back and pulling out of the driveway. I waved as he left, then put my bike back in the garage.

As I walked into the entryway, I could smell lamb stew with orzo pasta cooking. "Smells heavenly," I said coming into the kitchen.

Yia Yia smiled as she looked up from the pot of stew. "I know it's one of your favourites. Did you find anything for school?"

"Yep, I got a few tank tops and a pair of shorts. I ran into Lucas and his sister. He and I had lunch and talked for hours."

Yia Yia started to giggle. "That's nice, dear. I knew you two would get along."

I decided that asking her about the picture wasn't worth possibly upsetting her, especially since she was so happy right now, so I kept it to myself.

After supper, I trekked upstairs with Shade just ahead of me. I opened my backpack, pulled out my new clothes and threw them in my laundry basket to be washed. I put on my nightie and then lay on my bed. I was too tired to read, so I just put on a movie and fell asleep with Shade purring beside me.

CHAPTER

4

Sunday, June 13

The next morning, I texted Lucas: Hey Lucas. Still able to pick me up Monday?

Lucas: Yep. Be there bright and early.

Me: Thanks, really appreciate this. What are you doing for the rest of the weekend?

Lucas: Just hanging out with friends and probably going to Luna's archery tournament across town.

Me: Have fun ☺

Around lunchtime I noticed Yia Yia wasn't herself. She seemed troubled as she warmed up some soup for lunch. She pulled a bowl out for each of us but as she ladled some soup into my bowl, I saw she was tearing up.

"Yia Yia, are you OK?" I asked. I was really concerned. I couldn't bear seeing her cry. It was so out of the ordinary.

I think I had only seen her cry once before, and it was when one of her close friends passed away.

She turned and staggered to the stove. Hunching over she started to sob.

"Yia Yia, please. Please tell me what's wrong." I ran to her and threw my arms around her. Pleading with her to tell me, I took her face in my hands. She looked into my eyes, stricken with grief. Something horrible had to have happened.

"Oh, Ivy. I'm so, so sorry," she said in long laboured breaths. Shade came into the kitchen, sensing the tension. "Chloe . . . she didn't move away . . . she . . . she disappeared. She went missing," Yia Yia finished, taking in a deep breath before sobbing even more.

I froze. I felt my whole body lose all warmth as if all my blood was draining from me, pooling at my feet.

"Sweetheart, I'd rather you hear this from me," I heard Yia Yia's voice creek through her chest. My hearing was fuzzy. Everything sounded far away and muffled. I felt like I was surrounded by nothing. Like the kitchen wasn't even really there. Almost like being underwater. "I just heard on the news . . . Chloe was . . . found. Her . . . remains were found," Yia Yia cried.

My legs could no longer support me, and I sank to my knees. Yia Yia knelt beside me. She took me in her arms and pulled me close to her. I wanted to be sick. My best friend was dead. I started to shake, but I was still numb. I couldn't cry. I seemed to have forgotten how to. I couldn't feel anything emotionally or physically; I couldn't even think. We sat there on the floor, both losing ourselves in grief. Shade came and curled up between us. She always tried to comfort me; it was like she understood. But this was the worst pain I had ever experienced.

Slowly my feelings came back to me. Then I remembered how to cry ... and cry I did. I sobbed and hugged Yia Yia and Shade. We sat there for what seemed like hours, not saying a word, just sharing in the sorrow we all felt.

The sobbing slowly turned into crying, then to whimpering, then to a steady stream of tears. Yia Yia and I both lifted our heads from each other's shoulders and breathed in deeply as our bodies craved the air we had deprived them of for so long.

We wiped our eyes and pulled ourselves to our feet trying to steady one another. We both had the same idea, I could tell. Shade led the way and we solemnly walked to the den where we sat down together on the old worn leather couch with Shade between us again and reluctantly turned the TV to the local news station: "Construction workers recently uncovered a young woman's body near Blackwater Creek while digging the foundation for a new restaurant to be built there later this season. The body has now been identified as fifteen-year-old Chloe Ladas. She went missing a year ago and searches were called off four weeks later as the police and victim's friends and family had no leads as to her whereabouts. The victim went missing three days after her fifteenth birthday; she would have been sixteen this year. Police have not indicated the cause of death and are not available for comment at this time. I'm Sarah Borrows for Athenera's ATTV news."

Pictures of Chloe playing, blowing out her candles at her birthday and school portraits were placed on a continuous loop like a painful home movie. I felt like I was going to be sick again. I swallowed hard. "How could this have happened?" I thought. "She was so young. Who would kill someone so innocent?" My head hurt. Between the crying and the shock of what had happened, I was physically dizzy.

Yia Yia and I sat in silence ... stunned silence. There was nothing to say. Nothing could relieve this pain. Nothing could be done to change this. We couldn't even try to think of her last minutes as painless and quick. Nothing was known about her death yet, but I couldn't help but think the worst.

I couldn't hold it in anymore. I ran to the bathroom and threw up until I was empty and shivering from the trauma. I just wanted to curl up on the floor and disappear, but I had to try to be strong for Yia Yia. She was just as hurt as me. I had to try and get through this for her. Chloe was like a second granddaughter to her; she'd lived next to Chloe's family for so long. She was there when they brought Chloe home from the hospital and was always nice and so loving toward her. This was killing us both.

I came out of the bathroom just as there was a knock at the door. Shade had snuggled herself onto Yia Yia's lap, so rather than disturb them I answered the door. I didn't even bother to look in the mirror. I knew my eyes were red and puffy and my face was stuck in a twisted expression of disgust and confusion, but I didn't care.

It was Lucas. His expression was grim and serious. "I see you heard," he said sympathetically. "I brought you both dinner." He held up two grocery bags hanging from each wrist.

My lip started to quiver but I waved him in. He set the bags by the door and followed me into the den.

"Oh, Lucas, dear!" Yia Yia cried when she saw him. She rose from the couch and ran to him wrapping her arms around him. He hugged her back.

"*Syllypitíriá mou*. I know how much she meant to you," he said quietly.

"*Se efcharistó agápi mou*. It's really quite a shock. I've hoped for a year that she was OK. That she'd be found alive," she whimpered. Then she turned to me.

"Ivy, I really am sorry. I tried so many times to tell you she was missing, but it just never seemed like a good time and you were already dealing with so much … between how your mother is and the hectic life she created for the both of you. … But now that they found her body—"

"Shhh, it's OK, Yia Yia. I understand," I said.

Yia Yia kissed my forehead, then with trembling legs, she made her way back to the couch. I decided there was nothing more to learn tonight from the news. I doubted my stomach could have handled anything more. I went to pick up the bags, but Lucas stopped me.

"Ivy, please let me." I stepped back and let him pick them up, then followed him into the kitchen and sat down at the table. He glided around the kitchen pulling out plates, bowls and silverware for the three of us. He even put a bowl down for Shade and filled it with Ritzy Paté cat food. "I hope you don't mind if I join you. I brought enough for everyone," he said, setting the table.

"To be honest, I have no desire to eat . . . no offence," I said guiltily.

"I completely understand. You can eat when you're ready," he said, putting the containers of food in the fridge. "I'm not hungry yet myself."

After a few minutes of silence, we both travelled back to the den to check on Yia Yia. She had fallen asleep with Shade nestled beside her. I put her favourite throw blanket on them, turned down the TV and crept out, closing the big French doors behind me.

"Come up to my room. I want to let her sleep," I whispered.

We crept up the stairs and into my room. Then, I shut the door so we could talk freely and sat down on my bed. My legs still felt stiff.

"Do you want to talk about it?" Lucas asked, sitting beside me. I shook my head. There was still nothing to be said.

"I know I said it before, but I'm sorry. I haven't really dealt with death in a long time, but I know how it feels to lose someone close." He put his hand on my back and his warmth spread out to every part of my body. I leaned against him craving the heat. My body almost felt like ice and his touch was melting it. He wrapped me in his arms. I felt like I belonged there. I had never felt that before with any boy. I had had boyfriends before but nothing serious. I barely knew Lucas but his presence and empathy, his honest concern and his kindness all felt genuine, and I savoured it. I had had so little empathy in my life that my body's natural defence was to shut down and go numb. With Lucas, I could let my feelings go. He gripped them like a steel trap, obliterating the fear and uncertainty as his arms closed around me. I took my first deep breath since hearing the news. He smelled of sandalwood and tea tree oil and I drank it in feeling like I could shed my tension. I leaned deeper.

"You seem sleepy," he said into my ear. I nodded. He laid me back onto my pillow.

"Please don't leave," I said grabbing his wrist. "Can you please stay, just until I fall asleep?"

He sat down beside me and rubbed my back. "Of course, Ivy. As long as you want."

I felt so secure with him there that I wasn't afraid to fall asleep and dream. A few moments later I felt a faint kiss on my cheek, and I knew it was his.

CHAPTER

Monday, June 14

The next morning, I woke up rested and feeling slightly better considering the situation. Shade had slipped into my room, probably as Lucas was leaving, and was at the foot of my bed fast asleep.

The early morning sky was pale and grey, drenching my walls and floor in a gloomy sort of haze. It seemed fitting. Sitting up and looking out toward the woods, I saw little droplets of water clinging to the window. It was raining so hard I could hear it hit the roof. I loved the rain more than anything, and I especially loved it when it rained big, fat raindrops at night. It was so soothing to fall asleep to.

Not bothering to get dressed, I went to check on Yia Yia. She was still in the den but now sitting upright and glued to the screen watching the news.

"Morning, sweetheart," she croaked as I came and curled up beside her. "We are going to get through this. I promise."

"I know, Yia Yia. I love you," I said, kissing her cheek.

Yia Yia was still shaking. She had delivered Chloe when she was a nurse and she helped Chloe's mother, Maya, through her entire pregnancy. Yia Yia was that kind of person. Family and friends were extremely important to her and she seemed to have no ill will towards anyone. I wondered if Chloe's parents had found out yet. I didn't know them very well, as they worked a lot, but Yia Yia had always been around for us.

"I can't imagine what Poor Maya and Vasili are going through right now. No one should have to bury their child," Yia Yia said, shaking her head. "If only I knew how to reach them."

I hugged Yia Yia. "Is it all right if I hold off starting school for a couple of days? I really want to go, but I feel like a zombie and I don't know if I could concentrate with all the questions I already have crowding my head." I was already starting school extremely late in the year. There was only about a week or two left, but I wanted to try to make friends before the summer break. I would then also know who I would be in school with the following year.

"Of course, sweetheart. I completely understand. We both need time to grieve. Maybe later in the week would be a better time." She hugged me tight then disappeared into the kitchen. Probably to get us breakfast, in an attempt to normalize our lives again.

Nothing would be the same now knowing Chloe was dead. I would never forget it, and neither would anyone else who knew her. I tried to remember her as she was—happy, outgoing, funny and highly intelligent. She didn't flaunt her intellect though or look down on others who weren't as knowledgeable; she helped people. I remember one time I fell off my bike. I wasn't hurt but rather than run and get help she helped me up and brushed me off. Another time she saw a few younger kids stuck knee-deep in the muddy riverbed and started to dig them out while I got help. She was curious, and like a sponge, she wanted to suck up every bit of information about everything and anything. She loved to learn and teach what she knew. She taught me almost everything I knew about Greek mythology. We both had a passion for it and were always searching for myths we hadn't heard before. We used to spend hours in the town library pouring over every book they had on the subject; we must have read each a hundred times over. I smiled to myself. Remembering Chloe and the amazing person she had been was the best way to cope.

I went into the kitchen to share the story with Yia Yia hoping it would lift her spirits too. She was rummaging through the containers that Lucas had brought over yesterday, scooping *spanakorizo,* spinach and rice, and *souzoukaklia,* beef skewers, onto plates for us. It was clear Lucas had good taste.

"Oh no," I thought, "I totally forgot to let Lucas know I wasn't going to school. He's going to be here any minute." I pulled out my phone just as he pulled into the driveway.

"I'll be right back," I said to Yia Yia. I ran out to meet Lucas before he got out of his truck and hopped in the front seat trying to shield myself from the sun.

"Ummm . . . you look . . . nice?" he said, confused. I didn't look at all presentable.

"Yeah, I meant to text you. I'm going to stay home for a few days. I don't think I can focus on school just yet. I'm still really having trouble with the news about Chloe, and Yia Yia and I need time to mourn," I explained.

"That makes sense," he said thoughtfully. "How about I come over after school? Check up on the both of you?"

"That'd be nice," I said gratefully. He really seemed to care about us.

I waved as he drove off and watched him disappear down the hill.

Yia Yia had just sat down to eat when I came back in. I joined her but only had a few bites. I was still feeling nauseous and my stomach was still sore from vomiting. "I'm sorry," I told her, getting up to feed Shade. "I'm not hungry at all." I was unsteady getting to my feet due to a lack of blood sugar, and I felt lightheaded as I bent down.

"Ivy, honey," Yia Yia pleaded, "please try to eat a little more. You'll feel worse without food in your stomach and you'll stay sluggish. I know it's hard, and you'll feel this way for a while but please eat."

I ate slowly until she was finished then we threw the plates in the sink not bothering with washing them and retreated to the den.

I wanted to learn more about the case. There was no progression and the images that had burned themselves into my mind were ever-present. It was all too horrible to watch. I looked down and shook my head like an Etch a Sketch trying to erase it all, but I could still hear everything being said.

I stayed with Yia Yia until my phone beeped. It was Lucas texting to see if I wanted to get some fresh air. I wondered if Yia Yia would mind if I went into town with him. I ran my plan by Yia Yia. She thought it was a great idea, so I started up the stairs to shower and get dressed.

I pulled out my box of summer clothes and settled on a black tank top and grey jeans. I showered and texted Lucas. He said he'd be happy to go into town and joked that I hadn't missed anything terribly important at school. I went through my normal makeup routine of black mascara, eyeliner and bronzer then threw my hair up into a ponytail. I heard my phone chirp. It was no doubt Lucas texting, letting me know he was here. Saying goodbye to Yia Yia and kissing her on her forehead, I hurried out to the truck.

"It's good to see you," Lucas said solemnly noticing I was still a little shell shocked.

"You too," I said slightly blushing. "I've been thinking about the good times I had with Chloe and the way she was instead of the fact that she's gone," I said, somewhat smiling to myself. I had taught myself how to cope with grief, stress, fear, any unpleasant emotion. Sharron never tried to cheer me up or advise me to change my way of thinking, so I came up with my own strategy to deal with things in a healthy way. We drove into town and ended up at a home furnishings store. I needed curtains.

"How is Mrs. M holding up?" Lucas asked, concerned.

"She's still as upset as I am, but I think she's going to be OK in a few days. We both just need some time."

"That sounds like a good idea. The offer of a ride still stands when you're ready to start school."

"Thanks, I appreciate that. Luckily with summer weather starting early this year, I wouldn't mind riding my bike. I'll take you up on that ride on rainy days though.

"I love summer. It's my favourite time of year," Lucas said smiling. "I wish I could live somewhere where it was always summer."

His love of summer made me giggle. He was so passionate about it.

We browsed the aisles until I picked out some glittery purple blackout curtains and then Lucas drove me home. "If you or Mrs. M need anything just let me know. Day or night, whatever it is I'll do it," he said as he pulled up to my house.

"Thanks again, Lucas." He pulled me in for a hug and I surrendered, drinking in his ever-present heat and scent.

As I got out of the truck and walked to the house, his warmth slowly left my body, seeping out of every pore. The next few days dragged by with constant confusion and crying spells. There was still no progress in the case and no questions were being answered. No one seemed to know anything, even the police, and if the police knew, they weren't telling the public. Chloe and her parents had kept to themselves. They had no enemies, and no one could nail down a motive or even pinpoint the cause of Chloe's death yet. It was all speculation. With her parents still in the wind and without them around, I feared I would never find out what had happened to my best friend. With this thought, I decided school would be a welcome distraction. If I watched any more news, I would drive myself crazy.

CHAPTER

6

THURSDAY, JUNE 17

Thursday rolled around and I was ready to get back to reality and brave my new school. I texted Lucas Wednesday night to let him know I was ready to go back. He told me he'd pick me up at seven o'clock the next morning, giving us plenty of time for him to show me around.

I picked out what I was going to wear. In my mind, first impressions were especially important. I didn't want to look slutty, but I also didn't want to look stuck up or snobby. I settled on light jeans, a baby pink sleeveless deep neck top and a light white cropped sweater.

I had just finished putting my lip gloss on when Lucas texted. I took one last look in the mirror. I had attempted to perfect a thin layer of pink eye shadow. It turned out OK, but I knew I needed to practice that more. Otherwise, my usual eyeliner, mascara and bronzer were flawlessly applied. Satisfied, I ran downstairs to the kitchen, poured Shade her food, grabbed a carrot muffin, kissed Yia Yia, who was sitting at the table in her pyjamas, and barrelled toward the front door. I didn't want to make Lucas wait.

"Bye … love you," I called, heading out the door.

"Bye, I love you too."

I piled into the passenger's seat and set my bag down at my feet. "It's already so hot," I said peeling off my sweater.

"Yes, and I'm hating every minute of it," he said jokingly.

When we got to the school Lucas ushered me into the front office where I registered and got my class schedule.

"Let's see," Lucas said reading the schedule, "English, math, lunch, art and then a free period. Wow, your first semester is easy."

I agreed. English and art were my strong suits, and I could go home early every day. I hated math!

"I'll show you the English and art room," he said, handing back my schedule, "and your math class is upstairs in the south wing of this building."

After Lucas left me out front of my English class, I lingered outside the door a bit. I was so nervous. I had one friend in Lucas, but I was so anxious and eager to make more friends. I needed some girlfriends if I was going to feel comfortable here. Being friendly wasn't hard for me but starting a conversation and keeping it going was. I could never really think of anything to say past hello.

I walked in and headed straight for the closest seat to the back corner of the classroom. On the way, I passed by a group of about four platinum-blonde girls and heard them snicker. I kept walking trying to ignore the whispers and strange looks buzzing around me.

I should have expected it, being new and all, but I never really got used to it, even though I always seemed to be the new kid. The number of schools I had attended was staggering. I couldn't even remember half of them, and the only reason I had friends at my last school was that I had lived there the longest.

I slumped into my seat and tried not to notice all the eyes on me. Mr. Thompson, the English teacher, was a short and stout man with a big bushy mustache and thick-rimmed glasses. I opened my notebook and rummaged around my bag until I found a pen. As I was trying to keep busy writing the date on the top of the page, I heard someone sit down beside me. I looked up and snuck a quick look. A girl with sleek, long black hair, purple-tinged eyes, a swan tattoo behind her left ear and dark lipstick and eye makeup sat perfectly straight staring ahead. She had on black work boots, black jeans and a purple tank top with a thin black camisole over it. She wore several rings, including a nose ring, and had multiple piercings in her ears and lips. She was intimidating. My look must have startled her because when she noticed me, she jumped a little. I turned and smiled trying to be friendly, but she just kept staring straight ahead. Every so often throughout the rest of the class, I would see her glance sideways at me.

"Am I awkward looking?" I wondered. "What were those girls giggling about? And why did the girl with all the face bling look so startled by me?"

In an attempt to make some friends, I tried to talk to the face-piercing girl after class, but she bolted as soon as the bell rang. Then, trying to follow Lucas's crudely drawn map to the atrium for lunch, I bumped into an unbelievably cute guy. He had short brown hair, green eyes and a wide smile. He was tall and thin and wore tight-fitting jeans and a plain white shirt. There was a Celtic knot tattoo on his forearm.

"Slow down dare. What's de rush?" he sputtered.

"What?" I had no idea what he said.

"Got somewhere yer nade ter be?"

"Um . . . sorry, I'm not sure what you're asking," I said slowly, figuring he didn't understand me either.

"Is mise, Knox. You're juicy. Waaat is yisser name?"

He was Scottish or Irish. I think he said his name was "Knox," so I offered, "I'm Ivy."

He nodded then said, "Ope ter clap yer raun yer juicy las. Take 'er 'andy."

"OK," I said and hurried off.

That was a headache. I doubted I would ever be able to understand that guy, but I'd be lying if I said his accent wasn't cute. Even if I couldn't understand him, I would be completely content just looking at him.

I finally found the atrium and wandered in. I noticed Lucas sitting with a few other people on some stone benches by the far entrance. I hurried to join them.

"Hey, Ivy," Lucas said, standing up and smiling to greet me. "Let me introduce you to a few of my friends."

"That's Peter, Karel, Ian, Amy and Shanna," he said, gesturing to each person from left to right. "Guys, this is Ivy."

I nodded and they nodded back. I sat beside Lucas and mostly just listened to them talk while my eyes roamed the rest of the courtyard.

"Those girls over there"—he nodded to a group of girls, smiling and giggling, wearing cheerleading uniforms accentuating their skinny frames, with perfectly manicured nails and perfect hair—"they're the cheerleaders. The stoned-looking people over there are hipsters. And finally, we come to the neanderthal group over there. They make up the lacrosse team."

"Thanks. Very informative," I teased.

After lunch, I had art and my free period. Art class was uneventful, but I really liked my teacher, Ms. MacDonald. She was exotic and expressive when she talked. Because the school year was almost over each teacher just gave me a simple test instead of an exam like everyone else. They had gotten all my info from my old school and I guess I did well enough there that they felt comfortable passing me. I was glad I wouldn't have to repeat the grade.

I waited around for Lucas to drive me home after my free period and then finally the day was over.

At dinner that night I briefly described my day to Yia Yia. She had taken the day off to stay caught up on the news. No new information was given on Chloe's case. We found it infuriating that they hadn't seemed to have made any progress.

Frustrated, I turned my attention to an end-of-year assignment for art class. We weren't being graded so much as being assessed on our skill level at the end of the year. I tried to have fun with it as we were supposed to draw something we were passionate about. I decided to draw my depiction of one of the twelve gods or goddesses of Olympus. I scanned through my encyclopedia of Greek mythology and kept coming back to Aphrodite. There were so many ways she had been depicted, but I wanted to draw her as she would look currently, in trendy, fashionable clothes as a typical high school teenager.

I sprawled my notebooks out on the bed and started to sketch. As I did so, I thought about everyone I had met that day. Lucas's friends were nice, but I couldn't see myself having anything in common with them. They were all band geeks and seemed a little boring. I was desperate for friends, but I wanted friends who were . . . more like me, I guess. I decided tomorrow I'd try introducing myself to the girl with all the piercings in my English class. She was mysterious, which I found intriguing and exciting.

When my wrist got tired from drawing, I packed everything up for the night. Shade had pushed her way between me and my sketchbook anyhow, which meant she was ready for bed. And when she was ready, she made it clear that I had to be ready too. I got under the covers and started to close my eyes, still trying to work out what I was going to say to that girl the next day when I got a text. It was Lucas: Pick you up at 7:30 am tomorrow.

Me: Thanks. Nite.

He was so sweet, accepting and inviting. I wondered if I really need any other friends. Maybe just having him was enough. I was happy with him and school wasn't all about friends. If my attempt at making some girlfriends failed would that really be so bad? All these thoughts swirled in my head making it awfully hard to sleep. But with Shade's warm body curled up and purring on the pillow next to mine, I was soon in a deep dreamless sleep.

CHAPTER

FRIDAY, JUNE 18

My cell alarm went off an hour before Lucas was supposed to come to get me that morning. I opened my window to try and gauge the temperature. It was warm and the sun was only going to make it hotter. I decided I'd try standing out a bit today to try and make some friends. I looked through everything I had in my closet and finally grabbed a red tank top and dark jeans. I curled my hair in loose ringlets and wore a bold pink eyeshadow and lipstick. I then continued with the rest of my usual makeup routine.

When Lucas picked me up, he smirked at my appearance. "You look beautiful. Got a date?"

"Yeah, with your mom," I joked.

"My mom is dead," Lucas answered, completely deadpanned.

I felt the blood rush out of my head. "Oh my god, I'm so sorry," I breathed.

"Naw, I'm just kidding. I've never met her. Though I guess she could be dead." He laughed.

I still felt bad about my comment, but he didn't seem to mind, so I just made a mental note to never bring up his mom again.

We both laughed and carried on to school.

Walking into English class, I felt more confident this time. The snickering girls couldn't bother me today. I sat in the same spot as the day before and waited for face-piercing girl. Several minutes after class started, she scurried in, obviously embarrassed that she was late.

"Miss Nova Kazan," Mr. Thompson boomed, turning away from the chalkboard, "you know how I feel about tardiness in my classroom, young lady."

Nova nodded. "I'm sorry, sir," she began. "It won't happen again."

Her voice seemed to vibrate in my ears. Almost like it was shaking the earth. It was an uneasy feeling—not intimidation but more like cautious attraction.

She smiled sweetly at Mr. Thompson. Seemingly charmed, he brightened and turned back to the blackboard to begin the lesson again. As soon as his back was turned, she gave him the finger and sat down. A few people giggled, but he didn't seem to notice. Nova opened her books and started copying the lesson down as fast as she could to catch up.

I decided with Mr. Thompson being such a dick it wasn't the right time to try and start a conversation. It would likely get us both in trouble. Hoping she wouldn't run off after class like the day before, I pondered how to get her to stick around so I could introduce myself. Glancing around for inspiration, I noticed her purse on the floor beside her desk ever so slightly spilling into the aisle. Still scrambling to formulate a plan in the last few minutes of class, I stood just before the bell rang and pretended to trip over her bag as I started down the aisle. I strategically dropped my books.

"Oh, shit. Sorry about that. I really need to learn to keep my purse under my desk," she said, bending down to help me pick up my books. This time a different feeling washed over me when she spoke. A feeling of dread. An invisible force seemed to be holding me at the shoulders and pulling me back.

Today she was wearing a cropped, long-sleeved grey-and-purple floral v-neck top and high-waisted black leggings with the same work boots and same makeup style as the day before.

"No, it's my fault," I said trying not to sound like I had rehearsed it. "I'm so clumsy."

Stacking my books in my arms as I stood, she smiled and handed me what she had picked up. She was enchanting. She seemed to radiate confidence, which made me more comfortable. She was so cool and collected. Her smile made the dread suddenly wash away.

"You're new here, right?" she finally asked after a few painfully long moments.

I nodded.

"Well, I'm Nova."

"Ivy," I answered trying to match her poise.

"Met anyone else yet?"

"Oh, a few people here and there." I lied, thinking I'd sound pathetic if I told her I only really knew Lucas.

"I did bump into this Irish-sounding guy, Knox. He's pretty cute."

"I know what you mean. That accent drives me wild." She laughed. "Well, if you're not busy maybe we could have lunch together today. I could introduce you to my group of friends."

"That'd be nice, thanks," I said. Thank the gods, that was easy.

"OK. Meet me in the atrium, and then I'll take you to where we eat lunch," she said, hurrying off.

"OK."

I rushed to my locker, shoved my books in and dug out the map Lucas had given me. A few minutes later, I was standing at the entrance to the atrium. Nova walked up with another pretty girl beside her.

"Ivy, this is my friend Nikki," she said, gesturing to the girl beside her.

Nikki was platinum blonde with blue eyes and tanned flawless skin. Her hair was tied up into a tight bun and her perfectly manicured nails glittered silver with the slightest movement. She was wearing tight white leggings and a pink tank top peeked out from the slightly larger letterman's jacket she was wearing. She was equally as attractive as Nova if not a little more.

"Nice to meet you," she sang. She had a lyrical voice that almost sounded like it belonged in a princess movie.

"Come on, Ivy. We eat lunch by the statue in the art hall."

At the entrance to the drama, art and family studies wing of the school stood a large smooth-stone statue of a chimera. The fire-breathing, three-headed monster had one head of a lion, one of a snake, and another of a goat. It had the front legs of a lion, the hind legs of a goat and a long snake-like tail. It was frightening to look at, almost like it could come to life at any moment. Despite its ominous look, there was yet another pretty girl sitting at the base with her head resting on a guy's shoulder and the most beautiful girl yet was perched on the raised front paw of the beast swinging her legs and giggling with a beefy guy standing behind her with his arms around her waist.

"Hi, guys, this is Ivy," Nova called, gesturing to me.

"This is Jill and Bro," Nikki said, gesturing to the girl and guy sitting at the base.

Jill just nodded. She was pale with dyed red hair, brown eyes, dark makeup, dark navy jeans, a neon blue v neck tee and high-top sneakers. The guy beside her, Bro, was handsome with long wavy brown hair and dark blue eyes. He was tanned and slim but with a muscular build and an easy-going style. A green Polo and black jeans and sandals were all his outfit consisted of.

"Bro? His name is Bro?" I whispered to Nova.

"No one seems to know his actual name. Bro is just what everyone calls him," she whispered back.

"And that is Sythera and Marcus," Nova said, referring to the two on the statue.

Sythera was more enthusiastic. "Marcus," she said over her shoulder to him.

The familiar feeling of dread and the phantom force pulling me back returned and intensified as I stumbled backward.

Marcus came around to the front of the statue and effortlessly lifted Sythera to help her down. She looked like royalty. She was tall with long golden blonde wavy hair that reached her waist and had dreamy sea-blue eyes. Her nails were painted a soft light pink accompanied by tiny jewels lining the top of each nail, her skin was lightly tanned and almost seemed to glow. She was wearing a long white flowing skirt that reached her ankles and a light blue tank top with a white knit see-through camisole that was tied up to make it look like a crop top. Marcus was definitely part of some sports team. He was muscular, tanned and had dark features. He would have been handsome if it hadn't been for the scowl he wore anytime he looked at anyone but Sythera. He was wearing a school jersey, grey jogging pants and simple sneakers.

"So nice to meet you, Ivy," Sythera greeted me. She came over and hugged me tightly. "Oh sorry," she said when I tensed a little. "I believe a hug is the only way to welcome someone!"

"That's OK," I said a little stunned.

"You going to have lunch with us?" Jill asked, lifting her head.

"I thought it'd be nice to invite her," Nova chimed in.

Everyone nodded in agreement.

"We were just discussing what we should do this weekend," Sythera explained. "Nikki says we should have a party at my house. Jill says we should just go out for dinner. Do you have a suggestion, Nova?" she said looking in our direction.

"I like Nikki's idea of a party," Nova said.

"Me too!" said Bro. "Drinks and music and girls and—"

"No one asked you," Sythera interrupted. She looked annoyed.

"Sorry, hun. I have to go anyway," Bro said to Jill kissing her goodbye. "I'll call you," he called, strutting off down the hallway.

"Me too, princess. I love you," Marcus said in a low voice turning to Sythera. He kissed her passionately before jogging off, following Bro.

"I thought you and Bro weren't dating," Nikki asked Jill.

"I don't know what we are half the time if anything. I guess we are a couple this week."

I could tell the uncertainty bothered her, but it wasn't my place to pry. Sythera leaned against the statue and sighed dreamily, still reeling from the kiss.

"So, Ivy," she addressed me snapping out of her daze, "tell us a little about yourself. Did you move here with your parents? Where do they live? Is it just you?"

"Oh, uhh . . . I moved here to live with my grandma; she lives in the old Victorian house at the top of Aethon Hill, and yes, it's just her and me. My mom is living elsewhere with her husband, and I never knew my dad."

"Oh my, I'm so sorry," Sythera said, sympathetically putting her hand over her heart.

"It's fine. I don't remember him," I said, shrugging.

"Probably for the best. Parents suck!" Nikki said, making a face. "That's why I'm glad I don't have any."

Sythera's eyes went wild and she punched Nikki hard in the arm. Pushed sideways by the sheer force, Nikki steadied herself against the statute.

"What the—" Nikki started, but Sythera held up her hand to silence her.

"Maybe, Ivy wants her parents around. Did you ever think of that, you heartless bitch? You're so insensitive!" Sythera said through gritted teeth.

Nikki didn't retort. She just sat rubbing her arm. Her sexy smile twisted into a grim pout.

"Anyways," Jill carried on, taking the attention away from Nikki and Sythera. "What's this party for? We have to have a reason."

"She's right," Nova agreed. "We should have a theme."

"How about a costume party?" Sythera said. "Summer break starts in a few weeks. We could celebrate that."

Everyone nodded.

"Well, it's settled then. Next weekend I'll have a costume party at my place to celebrate the school year's end," Sythera clapped. "All of you should come to my place after school today to plan our costumes."

Everyone nodded in agreement again.

"There's still the matter of what to do THIS weekend," Nikki jumped in.

"How about the beach?" Nova chimed in.

"Oooh, I like that idea," Sythera mused.

"OK, then we will all meet there?" Nova asked, looking around.

Everyone including me agreed.

This was all moving so fast, but I was so desperate for my own set of friends. I didn't mind that someone else was taking the lead. I wasn't much of a leader in any of my other friend groups in the past. I was so grateful they were accepting and friendly.

After lunch, I went to art class and continued to work on my Aphrodite sketch.

"Ivy, that's very creative," Ms. MacDonald said, looking over my shoulder.

"May I?" she asked, gesturing to the drawing.

"Sure," I said, picking it up and handing it to her.

She studied it. "Aphrodite, I presume?"

"I wanted to try something a little different. I know the modern approach has been taken before by other artists, but there are so many depictions of what the gods looked like I just thought I'd show mine."

"It is very imaginative. Keep up the good work."

As Ms. Thompson was handing back my sketch, a sound from the corridor caught my attention. The classroom door was slightly ajar, and I could see Jill and Nikki in the hall. Nikki was visibly upset. Her shoulders were hunched, her back was arched, and she was baring her teeth, almost like she was growling at Jill. I could see Jill putting up her hands to calm Nikki down, but I couldn't hear what they were saying ... until Nikki suddenly screamed, "*Tha skotóso aftí ti sataniki skíla!*"

Everyone in my class heard her and a few people gasped. I suspected they knew what she had said because many of them spoke Greek, but I didn't understand.

"Ladies, shouldn't you be in class?" Ms. MacDonald said as she walked over and opened the classroom door slightly wider.

Nikki stood up straight and stared at her. Then her eyes slid to me and she and Jill both quickly walked away.

After school, I walked out to the parking lot to meet Lucas at his truck.

"Ivy!" Nova yelled, pulling up in her pickup truck. "Hop in. Sythera doesn't like to be kept waiting."

I had totally forgotten she wanted us all to be at her house to figure out the party details. "Oh, OK. I just need to let Lucas know. He's my ride," I said, looking around hoping to see him.

"Can't you just text him?" she asked anxiously.

I wondered how he'd feel if I bailed. In this case, he could go right home and maybe he'd be happy that I'd made some girlfriends.

"OK," I said climbing into the truck.

As we sped off toward the outskirts of town, I texted Lucas to tell him I was out with a friend and had my own way home. I texted Yia Yia to tell her the same. When we reached the countryside, I realized Sythera must live pretty far out of town.

"Why are you hanging out with Lucas? He's such a creep," Nova asked suddenly.

"What do you mean?"

"Lucas may seem like some golden boy but he's not who you think he is."

"He's the first person I met when I got here, and he's a good friend of my yia yia's."

"Do you like him?" she asked accusingly. She seemed almost disgusted at the thought.

"Well, he is cute, and he's been nothing but nice and inviting to me since we met," I said, trying to defend him.

"They always are," she said, rolling her eyes.

Nova pulled off onto a long winding driveway lined with lush olive trees. About two hundred yards in front of us I caught a few glimpses of an immaculate gothic roof towering over the already colossal wall of cypress trees that surrounded the house. We slowed as we came to a heavy iron gate. Leafy green vines encircled the twisted rods of the gate. It looked like the entrance to some secret garden. Nova pushed a button on the call box on the outer wall. We heard the gate unlock and proceeded through. We pulled up next to Sythera's pink Porsche which was parked just off to the side of the crescent-shaped gravel driveway. An Early Renaissance white stone fountain stood proudly in the middle.

We got out and I followed Nova up to the door and waited as she pushed a buzzer. A tired-looking, fragile petite old woman opened the door and bowed as Nova and I walked in. The foyer, more a ballroom, looked like something you'd expect to see in a castle from the nineteenth century. A tall and wide marble staircase gave way to three hallways. To the left was a short hallway leading to a set of double doors, to the right an equally identical set up, and straight ahead was a long hallway lined with multiple doors on either side with a bright pink one front and centre at the end.

Nova threw our school bags at the old woman, and she hurried away with them. Then Nova led us down the long hallway toward the bright pink door. She knocked, and we waited for someone to let us in.

"Finally," Jill said, answering the door.

"Sorry we're late," Nova said.

Behind Jill, Nikki and Sythera were sitting on a wooden canopy bed big enough for ten people. It was covered with several shades of pink blankets and over a dozen pillows. Sythera's room was gigantic.

"Wow, your room is amazing," I said as I scanned my surroundings. Besides the enormous bed, it had a big flat-screen TV and a chaise sofa with an armchair placed in front of it. One wall comprised four floor-to-ceiling windows and another wall was completely mirrored. There was a walk-in closest the size of my bedroom, and when I wandered over to the door on the far side of her room, I saw it led to an ensuite trimmed in gold. The beautiful vanity was strewn with high-end makeup, an earing tree, all kinds of brushes and sponges, hair accessories and countless expensive-looking necklaces which hung from the mirror frame. The air was heavy with the smell of peaches and clean linen.

"Yeah, it's all right," Sythera said, shrugging like she didn't live in an actual palace. "Come sit," she said, gesturing to Jill, Nova and me.

"Collette," Sythera said into an intercom on the side table.

In mere moments, the tired old women came in carrying a tray of chips, candy and cans of pop for all of us. She looked like she was made of brittle porcelain and that she would crack at the slightest movement. She set the tray on the bed and left without a word.

"So, anyone have any ideas for costumes?" Nova said, kicking off the conversation.

"It should be a group thing," Nikki chimed in. She looked like she had gotten over what happened earlier. Her sexy smile was back, and she was perfectly perched beside Sythera.

"Something everyone would know," Sythera said, "but that we can still make our own."

We all thought silently for a moment.

"How about something funny?" I offered. "There's this band called the Village People. They are all men, but they're always dressed up as different professions."

Everyone looked at each other; I don't think they had ever heard of them.

"I'll try to find a picture on my phone," I said, grabbing my cell.

I found one showing them all but then realized there were six members not five.

"That's perfect!" Sythera said when she saw the picture. "It doesn't matter that there are six. We can just pick and choose."

"OK, well who's going to be who?" Nova asked.

"I'll be the biker. I know I look good in leather," Sythera said.

"I'll be the cop," Nikki quickly said.

"I'll be the construction guy," Jill offered.

Nova and I scanned the picture. She settled on the cowboy, so that just left me to choose between the army guy and the chief. I chose army; it seemed like it would be easier to find something for that and it didn't seem right to dress up as a chief.

"Oh, my gods this will be so much fun," Nikki said, taking a sip of pop.

Everyone agreed.

"Of course, they will have to be the girl versions of whatever the occupation is, and they have to be sexy!" Jill said. "We have an image to uphold."

Again, everyone agreed except me, but I kept quiet. I meant for it to be funny, like with facial hair and everything. I guessed I could try to be an attractive "army girl," whatever that would look like.

"What's that?" Nova asked, gesturing to the floor behind me.

I looked to find the photo I had had in my back pocket. It must have slipped out when I took out my phone. Nova grabbed it before I had a chance to. When she looked at it, she suddenly went pale. I thought she might pass out. She swayed a little, and I got ready to catch her. She set down the photo and just stared blankly ahead.

"Nova? Are you OK?" I asked.

Everyone looked at each other uneasily. Sythera took the picture and scanned it. She looked surprised but had nothing close to Nova's reaction. "Cute guy. Who is he?" she asked simply.

"He may be my dad," I explained, trying to sound like I wasn't obsessed with it … which of course I borderline was.

That reveal made Jill and Nikki stiffen.

"What's going on?" I asked, annoyed. They clearly knew something I didn't about the photo or the man in it.

"Oh, Jill is part of a foster family and not really connected to her foster parents, and Nikki lives with one of her older boyfriends most of the time; she never knew her real parents. So any mention of parents kind of makes them uneasy. I don't know what's wrong with Nova. She's had a pretty normal upbringing, except her parents are dead and she lives with her mom's half-sister," Sythera said, trying to cover up the tension in the room.

Nova was still in a trance-like state, so to draw attention away from her Sythera started to go on and on about how wonderful Marcus was and how she was so in love with him. We ate and drank what Collette had brought us while Sythera talked about Marcus for what seemed like an hour. I had a hard time eating anything or paying attention to Sythera. I was worried about Nova. She had regained awareness a few minutes later but didn't say a word and kept her eyes glued to the picture, which was still lying on the bed in front of Sythera.

Before we left, I grabbed the picture and put it in my front pocket. I had to find a place to put this stupid picture where it would be safe. Nova slid off the bed, still visibly troubled. I could tell it was going to be a tense ride home.

I was right. All the way home, Nova didn't say anything or even look at me.

"See you tomorrow?" I asked hopefully when we pulled up to my house, but Nova just nodded and sped off.

The house was dark when I got home that night. Yia Yia was in bed, but she had left me a plate of dinner in the fridge. I wasn't hungry so I decided to go to bed as well. It was much later than I had planned to be home, but at least I didn't have anything else to do like homework.

I started upstairs when Lucas texted: Did I do something wrong?

Me: No, why?

Lucas: You didn't eat lunch with me and my friends today.

Me: Oh sorry. I met a girl in my English class. She invited me to have lunch with her and her friends.

Lucas: What's wrong with the girls I know?

Me: Nothing. I just don't have much in common with them. It's ok if we have a separate group of friends.

Lucas: Ok but promise me you'll be careful about who you hang around with.

Me: Umm . . . ok. Good night.

While I was changing, the photo of my mom and suspected father fell out of my jeans again. I unfolded it to study it more closely. There was something almost familiar about the man. Almost like I had seen him somewhere in a distant memory. I wondered if I asked Sharron if she would tell me the truth about who he was now that I wasn't living with her? I also wondered how much Yia Yia knew and if she would try to spare my feelings rather than bring up something painful if I asked. "I can't be in the dark any longer," I thought. "I need to know who he is."

Just as I got under the covers Shade pushed her way in and curled up at the foot of my bed in her usual spot. I didn't even have enough energy to turn my laptop on before I fell asleep.

CHAPTER

Saturday, June 19

The next morning, I packed a bag for the beach. The ocean lined the far side of town, so Yia Yia offered to drive me.

After about ten minutes of just wandering the beach, I spotted Sythera and the girls. Sythera, lying on an oversized hot-pink beach towel and wearing a white bikini and blue-tinted sunglasses, was literally shining. The sunglasses only made her eyes seem more intense. As she lay on her stomach chatting with the other girls, I noticed she had a swan tattoo on her lower back.

The other girls sat in a semi-circle around her. Nova, sitting on a dark purple towel to Sythera's left, was wearing a lilac-coloured bikini top dotted with small silver polka dots, grey skirted bottoms and thick-rimmed sunglasses. Next to her was Jill. She was sitting on a deep red towel and wearing a simple black one-piece with little white hearts and a deep plunging neck. Nikki was on Sythera's right sitting on a light blue overly plush beach towel. She was leaning back to display her perfect body in a light pink bikini that barely fit and matching pink-tinted sunglasses. She looked so content and confident. They all did.

"Have you seen Brett?" Nikki giggled. "I never considered him before, but he's sexy when wet," she said, staring intently at the group of wrestlers from school. "They all are. I'm going over there." Nikki said, standing and brushing herself off.

Sythera sat up and glared at her. "Uh, no, you're not."

Nikki shrank back to her knees. She looked wounded.

I tried to ignore the tension as I spread out my yellow towel. I felt I stuck out. My white daisy-patterned swimsuit didn't coordinate with my towel. I had just thrown a clean towel in my bag and I only had one swimsuit.

"Oooh, look, Ivy, there's Knox," Nova said, nudging me playfully.

Knox was walking down the beach shirtless and in tight neon yellow swim trunks lined with blue and orange triangles. With his swagger and the gaggle of girls trailing behind him, you could see him a mile away. His shorts were so visually loud that he was hard to look at for more than a few seconds. Only his incredibly chiselled features could draw your eyes away from them. His torso was so muscular and defined he looked like a statue of David.

"Lassies, how urr ye daein' th'day?" Knox said greeting us.

The girls looked confused. I was the only one who seemed to be able to loosely understand what he was saying.

"Good, thanks. Looks like you have quite the following," I said, gesturing to his fan club.

"They're hee haw compared tae ye sexy," he said, leaning toward me and winking.

I watched him walk away before I realized I was holding my breath.

"Oh, my gods he is totally into you!" Sythera laughed. "I could talk to him if you want. Maybe hint at inviting you to my party."

I blushed. He was incredibly cute, but I was kinda hoping to go with Lucas. Of course, I couldn't tell them that. They hated him.

"Come on, let Sythera help you. She is an expert on love," Nikki said excitedly.

"OK. Just don't make me sound desperate or anything," I said, suddenly panicking.

"Of course not," Sythera assured me.

"Scheming again, are we? Which poor soul is it this time?" said a condescending voice from behind me. I turned to see a tall, thin figure staring at me. She wore a hot pink bikini with gold chains hanging from the bralette to bring attention to her flat stomach. I recognized her as one of the cheerleaders I had seen in the atrium.

"Is there something you want, Joy? Or are you literally just here to be a bitch!" Nikki snapped.

"You know, I saw you talking to Lucas," she said to me, ignoring Nikki and kneeling beside me.

The other girls all glared at me. I uncomfortably inched away from Joy. I was so busted. I could feel my face flush.

"He's quite a catch. You better hold onto him tight; otherwise, Nikki will eat him alive," she said, looking from me to Nikki.

"Fuck off, Joy!" Nova said, jumping to Nikki's defence.

Joy stood up, momentarily startled. "Be warned," she said, regaining her composure and looking in my direction. "That slut will steal him." She spat and strode away.

"What the hell does she know?" Sythera snorted.

"She's just hurt that I stole Tyler away from her. He was the one who came onto me. I just indulged him," Nikki said innocently.

Sythera rolled her eyes.

"She's always had it in for us," Jill chimed in. "Pathetic."

"Joy … we do not like her," I thought, making a mental note.

CHAPTER

SUNDAY, JUNE 20

The next morning, I was anxious to talk to Yia Yia about the photo I had been carrying around in my pocket. I heard her in the kitchen making breakfast. After I set the table and we were both sitting down to eat, I unfolded the photo and laid it face up on the table.

"Come clean, Yia Yia," I said, pushing the picture toward her. "I need to know who he is."

Yia Yia picked up the picture. She closed her eyes and sighed deeply as she set it back down. "I wanted to spare you from this, Ivy, but I suppose you're old enough to know this now. Your mother was never one to stay in one place for long as you know. She was always sneaking out when she was a teenager and she fell in with a bad crowd. Despite my many attempts, I couldn't keep her away from them. She got into drugs and stealing and then she met … him," she said, pointing at the man in the picture. Her face was twisted in disgust.

"His name was Will. Your mother fell hard for him, but from the first moment I met him, I hated him. He was older than her by quite a few years, and it was sickening. I never knew how they met, but at the same time I didn't want to know." She turned the photo over as if she couldn't bear to relive the memory. "There was something wrong with him. His voice was sharp, his stance was strong and rigid, and his overall demeanour was nasty. He just sent out waves of rage and anger. I never knew what she saw in him, but I forbid her to see him and even went as far as to tell him to stay away from her. I knew if she stayed with him, she would end up dead—beaten to death or pushed into some life of crime that would kill her." She shook her head sadly.

"Sharron refused to leave him, so I secretly planned to have some friends come to stay with us to keep her safe and contained until he gave up trying to pursue her. The day before my friends were supposed to arrive, I found a note on the kitchen table. Your mother had run away with Will, and she didn't say where they were going. The note said unless I could learn to accept the way they felt about each other, I would never see them again. I gave some serious thought to what my life would be like without her. In the end, I had to accept her choice if I wanted to see her again."

I just sat there wide-eyed. The way Yia Yia was speaking about this man … I had never heard her talk about another person with such loathing.

"A week went by and finally I got a call from her. She still wouldn't tell me where they were, only that she was safe and would be back soon. After a handful of calls over a span of five months, she finally came home.

"I remember sitting here at the kitchen table. She was standing in the doorway with her hands pressed against her pregnant belly and tears rolling down her cheeks; Will had left her. She was crushed, but I promised I'd help her take care of you and that I'd always be there for her and you. I've never broken that promise. Four months later, I helped deliver you here at the house and the rest you know."

"Will is your father, Ivy." She put her face in her hands, and I saw I single tear drop from between them. "I don't know what happened to him and I don't care. I told you this because you deserved to know, but I'm going to ask that you don't go looking for him; he's dangerous. I wasn't able to keep your mother away from him, but I will not give up again and lose you to him as well."

I sat for a moment taking in all of what Yia Yia had said. I was only shaken out of my daze of disbelief when Shade rubbed up against my leg. When Yia Yia raised her head, her eyes were full of hope, and I just couldn't deny her request. It was probably impossible to find him anyway, and if what she said were true, he was clearly an asshole. For all I knew he could be dead by now. I had little information to go on.

"Thank you for telling me, Yia Yia," I said taking her hands. "I won't go looking for him . . . I promise."

She nodded as a few more tears rolled down her cheeks. After a few minutes of silent reassurance, we sat back and slowly started to eat.

I had to call someone. I couldn't hold all this new information in. I thought about calling Nova but was worried she may not understand the severity of the situation since she had been adopted. Then I thought about calling Sythera; her parents were never around so she might understand the sense of abandonment I felt. But I hadn't told her about my mother's life with me before I moved here. It would be a lot to explain all at once. Lucas was the best choice. He knew my back story and about the photo and my doubts.

I texted him that I needed to talk, and he came to pick me up. I let Yia Yia know that I wouldn't be late and left as quickly as possible so she wouldn't have time to ask any other questions. I think deep down she knew I was leaving to talk to someone about my father, but I think she also knew I needed to talk about it to come to terms with it.

"So, my suspicion was right," I started as we set off. Lucas began driving up the road toward an overlook on the edge of a cliff. Chloe and I had always snuck up there to play until someone had fallen off the cliff and died. Then we were forbidden to ever go up there again.

"What about?" Lucas asked.

"The guy in that photo I showed you … Yia Yia confirmed it. He's my father."

I saw out of the corner of my eye Lucas's grip on the steering wheel tighten.

"How do you feel about that?" he asked, visibly concerned.

I thought for a moment. How did I feel about it? I was angry, sad, confused. I felt incomplete. It was as if there were a whole chapter of my life missing and I would never know what had happened during that time.

"I don't know," I finally said. "She told me he was horrible and to not go looking for him. I told her I wouldn't, but I wish I knew more. In the past, any time I asked Sharron about my father she would get really angry and ignore me. I guess I'll never know anything about him. All I have to go off of is what Yia Yia told me."

"I would trust her. … She has no reason to lie to you," he said, pulling into the empty dirt parking lot.

The town was beautiful from up here.

"I really never gave him much thought. I honestly believed I'd never find him or know anything about him. But now that I do know a little it raises more questions. Like why did he leave Sharron? Did he know she was pregnant? Was I the reason he left her? Did he love me? Does Sharron love me? Was I really just a horrible mistake?"

My eyes started to water. I knew I wasn't planned but knowing my dad left before I was even born stung. He didn't even stick around to meet me.

I turned my head trying to hide my overwhelming urge to full-out cry. I grabbed onto the leather seat on either side of me and bore down. Tears started to fall, and my shoulders shuddered.

All at once, I felt Lucas's hand on my back and my body flooded with warmth. He grabbed my chin gently and turned my head toward him. His eyes were soft and sincere.

"I know how it feels when you're unsure if you're loved or not. But your yia yia loves you, and . . . I think . . . I do too," he said, wiping away my tears with his thumb.

I searched his face for any indication he was joking. He hardly knew me. Love wasn't possible this soon.

Almost as if he could read my mind he said, "I know that seems crazy, but I just have this irresistible need to protect you, to be with you. I have no fear when I'm around you and I find myself awestruck by your beauty. Inside and out. You're genuinely a good person, and the world needs more people like you. Who couldn't love you?"

I didn't think I would ever hear everything I had wanted to be told my whole life, all in one moment.

I was speechless. Shocked. "Is this for real?" I wondered.

"Ivy . . .?"

I forced myself to look into his eyes. His mesmerizing gaze made me feel safe and a little more at ease.

He leaned closer to me, his scent invading my senses. He grew closer and closer until his lips were inches from mine. "I love you, Ivy," he whispered, and then he kissed me.

Electricity pulsed through me. Everything around us fell away. Every worry, fear, doubt I ever had was gone. He pushed harder and I pushed back. I didn't want the feeling to end. I wrapped my arms around his neck, and he pulled me closer to him by my waist. I straddled his lap not breaking the kiss. I felt like I might shatter if I were to stop. I couldn't get enough of his touch. The heat, the passion I felt. I pressed my hands against his chest. His hands fervently trailed up my arms grabbing both my hands in his. He then guided my hands to his shoulders and gently pulled back. I kept my eyes closed in suspense; I waited for him to start again, but he didn't. I opened my eyes, feeling suddenly embarrassed, and slid back into my seat. We were both quiet, and the tension swiftly grew heavy in the confined space.

He turned off the truck and slipped out of the driver's seat. I watched him walk toward a withering laurel tree leaning precariously close to the edge of the cliff. I scrambled out of my seat and followed him. His hand was pressed into the tree's bark. I looked and could see it was covering a faint carving.

"Did you mean it?" I questioned.

He glanced at me over his shoulder.

"Did you mean it? When you said you loved me . . . did you mean it?" I pushed.

His shoulders sagged and he hung his head, almost as if he were ashamed. I started to tremble, dreading his answer, afraid he would retract what he had said. He slowly turned and lifted his head.

"Of course, I meant it," he sighed. "I'm confused. I have a lot going on and a lot to think about."

That sounded like an excuse for his actions. It was almost as if he were breaking up with me even though we weren't even dating.

His hand slid down, revealing the carving. It was a heart with an arrow through it. It read "Lucas + Daphne forever."

"Take me home," I said, deadpanned.

He just nodded. We got back in the truck and descended the hill in silence. Once home, and with an implied goodbye, I hurried inside and ran straight up to my room. I had been able to hold off while in the truck but almost immediately as I reached my bedroom door the tears fell.

Stripping down, I got into the shower and let the warm water mix with my tears. I was unable to stop crying. I started to sob and took pathetic comfort in the fact that no one could hear me. I wasn't sad; I was angry. The tears felt like fire running down my cheeks and burning my face. Raw rage felt almost good to let out. Who was Daphne? And if he was so in love with her where was she now? Lucas was the only person besides Yia Yia I thought I could trust. He just betrayed that trust when he led me on.

I wished I could talk to Chloe. She had always been easy to talk to. She never judged me and was so mature beyond her age. I tried to think of what she would say, but we had hardly talked about boys when she was alive so I couldn't fill in the blanks. I had planned to go over to her house to search it, but things kept getting in the way. This didn't help.

All these questions about my father and Lucas's indiscretion and now thinking again about Chloe gave me a pounding headache. I stood under the water in the shower until it turned cold. Then, wrapping a towel around myself, I stood in front of the mirror and stared in disdain at my reflection. I had fallen for him; I had fallen for him hard, and it had completely blown up in my face. I let my guard down when I should have been building it up from the moment I met him. The tingle I had felt from his kiss still stung my lips. Spitting and grabbing a washcloth, I scrubbed my lips until I felt the first layer of skin peel off. My legs were stiff and weak; I walked to my bed trying to steady myself against the wall. Not bothering to put anything on, I got under my blankets and continued crying until I fell asleep.

CHAPTER

10

I woke up two hours later to my phone dinging. It was a text from Nova: Hey, come shopping with me. I need to get stuff for my costume.

My head was still pounding; I lay back on my pillow and thought. "With only one high school in town, chances are she knows who Daphne is, so maybe she can give me some insight on what his deal is. What he's been like with other girls." I decided I really needed some girl time.

Nova: Meet me at the Bean.

I realized I could really use some coffee too, so I agreed to meet her.

I reapplied my makeup, threw my hair up into a messy bun, and asked Yia Yia if I could borrow the car. Driving into town, the air was much colder than it had been a few hours previously. Dark, menacing storm clouds were gathering on the horizon.

I parked at the Bean, ordered myself a butterscotch frap and got us a table while I waited for Nova.

I looked around and I recognized a few people from school, mostly in little clusters with many of the same people they hung out with at school except one guy. I looked a little harder at him and realized I had just locked eyes with Knox. He noticed me, got up and walked over to my table with that wide smile as he had done before.

"Awright thare. Kin ah jyne ye?" He asked, pulling out the chair across from me.

I nodded assuming he asked if he could sit.

"How urr ye?" he said, setting his coffee down.

I did my best to decipher his slang. "I'm OK. Just waiting for Nova. We are going shopping for our costumes for Sythera's party next weekend."

"That's crakin'. Ah ken her she's gey bonny," he said, winking.

I nodded.

He gave a little laugh. "A'm aff tae that pairtie tae. Ah wull see ye thare," he said, getting up. Just then Nova walked in and saw me talking to him.

I smiled and waved. Knox winked at her and swaggered over toward the group of cheerleaders. Like everyone else, they loved his accent.

"Do I hear wedding bells?" Nova joked, sitting down across from me.

I looked over at Knox. "He's cute, but there is that language barrier."

Nova laughed. "I don't know . . . I like the accent."

I thought for a moment. I wondered if Lucas was going to the party. Why did I care if he was? Maybe going with someone else was a better idea anyway.

"You seem unsure," she said carefully.

"Well, I was into someone else, but we just had a bit of a fight," I said, unsure I should even be telling her.

"Oh, who is it?" she said with a smile. She clearly knew there was more to the story.

"Lucas Teresi. He has his old girlfriend's name carved on a tree up at the look-off. I thought he liked me, but he doesn't seem to be over her," I said with a frown. Even saying his name gave me a bad taste in my mouth.

Her eyes went wide. "Well, you dodged a bullet there. He's a total player. He did the entire female population of the school and two guys that I know of."

I was stunned. He didn't seem that kind of person. Skeptical, I changed the subject.

"Where did you want to go to get your costume?"

"The thrift shop," Nova answered. "It's just for one night, so I thought no need to spend too much on it."

I nodded. "Good idea. I'll probably get my stuff there too."

As we made our way to the thrift shop, I carefully probed Nova for more information about Lucas. Even though she obviously hated him, maybe she knew some things Yia Yia didn't.

She told me how he had cheated on almost every girl he had been with and that he was a crazy stalker. Surprisingly, she knew who Daphne was too. According to her, Lucas stalked her and was ridiculously in love with her.

I froze. I hoped she was mistaken. "I can't even imagine him doing something like that," I thought. "And if Nova knew about this, it was probably common knowledge … but Yia Yia would never knowingly be involved with someone like that."

"Hey, it's OK," Nova said, snapping me out of my thoughts.

I realized I had stopped in the middle of the sidewalk.

"The girls all know what he's like. Sythera, Nikki, Jill and I will keep you safe from him."

"Thanks," I said still shook. This was just too much. "How could I have been so wrong about him?" I wondered. "I have to ask Yia Yia about this when I get home."

Nova and I pawed through several racks of clothes in the thrift shop looking for anything we could use as a costume. She found a cow-print mini skirt and a red shirt with a rope design around the collar.

"I have cowboy boots and a hat at home, so I'm finished. Let's look for your stuff now."

We looked some more and found camouflage-print shorts. Since there wasn't much else, I just choose a black tank top. Lastly, we found an old hat that looked like it had probably been used in the military at one point. It was faded and dark green, almost the perfect match to the green on the shorts.

After we paid for our purchases Nova offered me a ride home.

"No thanks. I drove my yia yia's car here."

"OK, well what about next week? I can pick you up early and we can all get ready at Sythera's house."

"Yeah, that'd be great. Thanks."

"Expect a text from your date tonight," she called, getting in her truck.

I waved and walked back to my car.

Suddenly I saw something duck behind one of the other cars close to mine. I first tried to ignore it thinking it was just an animal or my imagination but then I saw it again and got a better view. It was unmistakably a person, and it was stalking me. It was whatever I had been seeing in the woods and at my window in the past few weeks. Not letting whoever it was get away again, I sprinted to the spot where I had seen it. Nothing was there, but then out of the corner of my eye, I saw someone dodging and weaving around the rest of the parked cars.

"Leave me alone!" I screamed out after it.

The figure stopped and turned at the edge of the parking lot. I could see the silhouette of a girl with long dark hair. I couldn't see any other defining features from that far away in the dark. Then she took off running again into the woods behind the lot. I got into the car and locked the doors. I called Yia Yia on the way home and stayed on the phone with her until I got there. I told her what I had seen, and she said it was right to call her.

She locked the door behind me as I rushed into the house.

"Are you OK? I thought you were with a friend," she said, hugging me tightly.

"I was. This happened after she had left. I was walking to my car and I saw her."

"Do you have any idea who it might be?"

"No. I'm almost certain it was a girl. It's not much to go on."

"I'll call the police," she said, getting up to get the phone.

"No, Yia Yia. Like I said, I don't have the slightest idea who it was, and they haven't done anything illegal or anything to hurt me, so let's not get the police involved. There isn't anything they can do."

She stopped mid-dial and hung up. "Maybe you're right. But from now on don't go anywhere alone, especially at night." She hugged me goodnight. "And please lock your window tonight . . . just in case."

This threw a wrench in my plans. I planned to go over to Chloe's after Yia Yia went to bed, but now it didn't feel safe enough. Once again, something came up to stop me from going over.

I made my way upstairs. Shade could tell I was on edge when I got to my room and curled up next to me as I sat on my bed. She seemed concerned, and I gave her a little scratch to assure her I was OK. I was too distracted by what had just happened that I totally forgot to ask my yia yia about Lucas. I would get the information from her eventually. Until then, I decided I would keep an open mind.

CHAPTER

Monday, June 21

The next morning, Nova texted me again: Hey. Sythera wants to hang out at the lookout after school. Meet us there.

I was a little offended. Nova knew that Lucas and I had fought about the tree there. That's the last place I wanted to be. I figured reminding her was pointless since they all seemed to do whatever Sythera wanted anyway, and it wasn't Nova's idea; so after school that day, I got dressed and started the hike. I was dying from the heat by the time I got to the top of the hill. It was stupid of me to walk, but Yia Yia was out with the car and I really had no other way; Nova and the girls had been absent from school all day, and biking would have been just as bad if not worse.

"Ivy!" Nova called from a picnic table. I waved and tried to look like I wasn't exhausted.

"Here, we brought you a smoothie," Jill said, sliding a takeout cup toward me.

I gratefully took a long sip and savoured the feeling of cold pomegranate slush running down my parched throat. I thanked them, and as I sat down, I glanced at the tree. The heart with Lucas and Daphne's names burrowed into my thoughts. The girls must have noticed because Sythera came and sat down next to me.

"Where were you guys today?" I asked. "If they had ditched," I thought, "why didn't they tell me?"

They all exchanged glances and then Sythera said, "I had a lengthy hair appointment."

"My boyfriend wanted me to stay in bed with him," Nikki laughed.

I looked at Jill.

"Bro was hungover and I stayed at his place to take care of him," she said.

"I just couldn't deal with Mr. Thompson today," Nova said when I turned my gaze to her. "I was going to be late and I've had my fill of detention this month."

I guessed that all checked out. If they weren't telling me the truth, there wasn't much I could do about it anyway.

"I called Knox for you. He should text you soon to ask you to my party," Sythera sang excitedly, changing the subject.

"Thanks," I said, trying to fake excitement. I was lousy at it.

"Nova told us what happened," Sythera said, trying to meet my eyes. "I'm sorry that happened, and I wish we would have known that you liked Lucas. Maybe we could have saved you all this heartbreak. I promise he's nothing special. You're better off without him."

I couldn't look at any of them. I kind of felt ashamed that I hadn't told them, so I just kept my eyes down.

"We do think you should know the whole story though," Nikki said from behind me.

I gulped down more of the smoothie and nodded, even though I wasn't sure I wanted my image of Lucas to be tainted any further. What if I decided to forgive him?

"So, Ivy, I told you that Lucas was in love with this Daphne girl," Nova started. "Not sure why he was, but that doesn't matter. She liked him too but not nearly as much as he liked her. He was becoming obsessive and clingy so she broke it off, but he couldn't move on. He kept following her and begging her to get back together with him, but of course, she refused as any sane person would do." Nova rolled her eyes.

Sythera jumped in. "He kept calling her and texting her and eventually would unexpectedly show up at her house. Then one day he cornered her at school and told her he couldn't live without her and that he would do something drastic if she didn't give him another chance. After a few months he literally drove her crazy. Then, one night in some kind of fever rage, Lucas chased her up here and she fell off the cliff right by that tree."

My mouth dropped open. I couldn't believe what I had just heard. He had driven Daphne literally insane and forced her to throw herself off a cliff just to get away from him? This was crazy. This had to be some kind of joke or horrible rumour. It couldn't be true.

Almost as if they were reading my mind, Jill said, "I wish we were making this up, but it's all true."

"He was clingy when I dated him too," Sythera confessed.

My head shot up and I stared at her. "You dated Lucas?" I asked slowly.

"Very briefly. I didn't know any of that when we started to date and that was before Marcus came here," she explained.

"Yeah, she even had a one-night stand with Lucas's best friend before Marcus showed up," Nikki laughed.

"Shut the hell up, Nikki!" Sythera screamed.

Nikki scurried back and almost fell backwards off the picnic table.

"You ever mention that again and I will make you regret it," Sythera growled.

She regained her composure and turned back to me.

"From now on you can't hide anything from us if you don't want to get hurt. We are your friends, and we would never steer you wrong," Sythera said grabbing me in an awkward hug. Her vanilla perfume stung my eyes and worsened my already wicked headache. It smelled like she bathed in it. I half-smiled and for the rest of the evening, we just sipped our drinks and talked about the party.

When I got home, Yia Yia was sitting in the den reading. Shade was stretched out beside her.

"Ivy ... what's wrong?" she asked.

I knew I looked upset. The information about Lucas didn't make sense. I needed to clear this up with her. Even though Nova and the girls were my friends and I trusted them, I needed to hear if there was another side to this story.

"I was told some pretty disturbing things about Lucas today," I said, sitting down. I fidgeted with the tassels on one of the throw pillows while I tried to figure out how to ask her about what the girls had told me. "How well do you know Lucas?" I asked carefully.

"I've known him a very long time."

"Did you know his girlfriend Daphne?"

"Is this about her death, Ivy?"

I nodded.

She took my hands in hers and made sure I was looking her in the eye. "I don't know who told you what but I'm only going to explain this once, and I don't want it to ever be spoken about it again, understand?" she said in a firm, serious voice.

I nodded again.

"Lucas did once have a girlfriend named Daphne. She was a nice girl but very mentally unstable. Lucas loved her very much. For some reason, she broke up with him, but they remained friends. He knew about her inner demons and would check up on her almost every day. Then it got to the point where she stopped answering her phone, so he would go over to her house to make sure she was all right. He begged her to get help several times, but she refused. Sensing she was going to do the unthinkable, Lucas followed her to the look-off point one night and before he could stop her, she threw herself off the cliff. It nearly killed Lucas. He is a very loving person, Ivy. I trust him with my life, and you should too. He will keep you safe, and he is very loyal. Everyone has their secrets. You don't need to know everything. Some things are better to just let go.

I breathed a sigh of relief. Yia Yia's version seemed a little more plausible than the crazy stalker story the girls had told her.

I thanked her and vowed to never speak about it again. I decided not to mention my conversation with Yia Yia to the girls. They were just trying to protect me and maybe they had heard their story from other people who had it wrong. I thought it best to just keep my ex-friendship with Lucas and my friendship with them separate.

CHAPTER

Tuesday, June 22

I didn't hear from Knox until the next morning. Luckily, he didn't text like he talked. He told me his costume was a secret and that I should try to find him at the party. I thought that'd be interesting, so I agreed.

To kill time, I decided to work on my sketch of Aphrodite for art class. Anything was better than racking my brain about Lucas and sketching always calmed me, but my mind soon floated to Sunday night and the person who had been hiding in the parking lot. I thought about all the girls I knew and none of them seemed to fit her profile. No one had anything against me that I knew of. I'd hardly been there long enough to piss someone off. I considered Joy or one of the other cheerleaders, but it wouldn't make sense for any of them to follow me.

Shade pushed her way onto my lap and lay right on top of my sketch. She decided I was done, but I really had to keep working. I provided a distraction by letting her outside and then set myself up on a window seat where the light was good and got back to work. Aphrodite's face was the hardest part. I wasn't sure which expression to give her. I wanted to give her something no one had ever given her in any other painting. As I drew, I started thinking again about the girl in the parking lot and what she might look like in the light. My drawing started to look like a sinister "mean girl," almost like someone I'd seen before. Maybe in a past life. It was easy drawing Aphrodite's face after that. Once I gave her a kind of personality the rest just fell into place. Satisfied, I took a break to get something to eat.

As I was searching in the fridge, I got a text from Lucas. I wasn't ready to talk to him, so I ignored it while I fixed my lunch. He had a lot of nerve texting me after what he'd done. But with the new information I had, I decided I would hear him out.

As I ate, the temptation to see what Lucas had texted was starting to take over; I couldn't think of anything else. I checked to see what he had said. If it was anything less than an apology, I wasn't going to text him back.

> Lucas: I'm sorry about what happened Sunday. I don't regret kissing you, but I do regret leading you on. I don't think we should see each other anymore.

> Me: When did I ever give you the indication I wanted a serious relationship? I never wanted anything more than a friendship.

> Lucas: We both know that's not true. Look I'm apologizing. I still love you but not with everything I am and that's not fair to you.

Me: What are you even talking about? If you really love me, you have a funny way of showing it. I know all about Daphne and I want nothing to do with that nonsense.

Lucas: You know NOTHING about Daphne. I know you asked Nova and she doesn't know anything either! Out of all the people you could have befriended you choose those bitches.

Me: Don't talk about my friends like that! I KNEW you were the one stalking me! Leave me alone!

Lucas: What are you talking about? My friend Rooster overheard you two talking about me when he was downtown yesterday. That's how I found out. Wait, is someone following you?

Me: Like you care! You don't keep things from friends, and if we aren't friends anymore then I have nothing left to say to you.

Lucas: Whatever Nova said is completely false! I'm not a bad guy, I'm just dealing with a lot right now.

Me: I trust Nova more than I trust you right now. Everything you're saying is such a cop-out.

Lucas: Who is following you? You have to tell me so I can help you.

Me: Goodbye, Lucas. DON'T EVER TEXT ME AGAIN!!

Lucas: Whatever! I can't protect you from yourself. Nova and all those other girls are horrible and will say anything to turn you against me and anyone else they don't like. I can tell it's worked so far. Of course you can't see it's all a manipulative trick. Trying to be your friend was the biggest mistake I've ever made.

He sounded like the charming bad guy from a soap opera. How could I ever have feelings for someone like that? I hated myself for falling for him. I texted Nova. I had to get out of the house before Yia Yia asked me what was wrong. She was such an advocate for him, and I didn't want to bring her into it. I knew anger was written all over my face. Nova said she'd be right there. I quickly let Shade back in and ran upstairs to my room to bask in the sun shining through my open window.

"Bye,YiaYia,goingoutwithafriendbebacklaterbye." I spouted off the sentence so quickly I don't think she understood or even knew I was leaving. I sent her a quick text and she amazingly wrote "have fun" and left it at that. I was so grateful she didn't ask any questions.

Nova had stopped at the end of the driveway and looked genuinely concerned when I got into the passenger seat. "Are you OK?" she asked.

"I need to get out of here. Can we go somewhere and talk?"

Nova thought for a moment. "I have just the place."

She turned and started down the hill. We drove through town and out to the countryside. The houses started to get farther and farther apart from each other and soon there was nothing but run-down farms, fields of plowed crops and a few clusters of cows. We turned down a remote dirt road. It was lined with trees and almost felt like a cave as the branches full of lush leaves stretched across to meet the branches on the opposite side. The road came to a dead-end and just to the left was an old haunted-looking farm. The old house looked abandoned and the barn looked like it was missing a few boards and shingles.

"What are we doing here?" I asked.

Nova parked and turned off the vehicle. "I've always loved this place. I like to daydream that I live here. I'd have a bunch of farm animals, like chickens, cows, maybe a horse or two and never have to worry about anything. Just take care of my animals, spend my afternoons riding in the open fields and raise a little family with Jason. I dream we have four or five kids. Three boys and two girls or two of each."

I could imagine her doing that. As she talked, she seemed almost sad as reality trickled back into her mind.

"Who's Jason?" I asked.

"Oh yeah, I guess you haven't met him yet. Jason's my boyfriend. He's away at a lacrosse tournament. Luckily, he'll be back for the party. He's great. I think he could be the one."

She seemed to slip into a daydream as she started toward the house.

"So why the need to get out of the house?" Nova asked shaking her head to snap herself out of her daze.

"Lucas," I sighed.

"But I thought you weren't going to talk to him."

I thought telling just her was OK. I trusted her. I knew I had planned to keep my friendships separate, but I had to confide in someone. There was no middle ground. Be it her or Yia Yia, they were biased.

"I never said that, and my yia yia told me that whole situation between him and his ex was a mistake. That the way it happened wasn't how you said it did."

Nova stiffened. She looked angry.

"I'm not calling you a liar. Just maybe whoever told you what happened was speculating."

Nova nodded. "Maybe. Though the other stuff I told you is true. He is a player and a creep."

"I didn't ask Yia Yia about that. I doubt she would think that anyways."

The rest of the time we were mostly silent. I tried to forget the fight and join in a daydream about Nova's little farm. But in every vision, I was with Lucas. Was I ever going to be able to get him out of my head?

When Nova dropped me off at Yia Yia's later she assured me that after my falling out with Lucas she would take over driving me to school if I couldn't borrow Yia Yia's car. I thanked her and hurried inside.

"Did you have a nice time?" Yia Yia asked. She was sitting in the kitchen now.

I nodded. "I just went out with a friend to talk. I'm kinda tired so I'm going to get an early night."

"OK, love you. Good night."

I gave her a kiss and hurried upstairs.

It wasn't a lie; I really was tired. The outing had helped but not as much as I had hoped. My head was still buzzing. Shade tried to offer some comfort by lying down and purring beside me. I changed and instead of turning on my laptop I just pulled the covers over my head.

CHAPTER

Wednesday, June 23

I was up and wide awake by six because I had gone to bed so early. I showered, got dressed and actually had time to sit down and have breakfast with Yia Yia and Shade. I felt slightly better after such a nice long sleep, and it was nice not having to rush. Nova had texted me that'd she be there for seven thirty, so I just hung around and chatted with Yia Yia. Considering I hadn't spent very much time with her since school had started, it was long overdue.

Me: It's 8:00! Where r u?

Nova: Be right there.

"We are going to be so late," I said dropping into the passenger side when she finally got there. "You said seven thirty. Where were you?"

"I'm sorry. The Bean screwed up my coffee order, but I got one for you." She gestured to the other cup in the console's cupholder.

I didn't drink black coffee, but she was nice enough to think of me, so I politely sipped the bitter drink until we got to school then threw most of it out before we got into the English hall. We were super late and even though we ran, we had to wait out in the hall awkwardly until Mr. Thompson chose to let us in. Some teachers did that; they would make you sweat out the inevitable detention we knew we were both going to be slapped with.

"You may come in now. I'll see you both at lunch today for detention," Mr. Thompson said, looking down his nose at us. As Nova and I slunk to our seats she gave me a "what a dickhead" look. I stifled a giggle and winked.

"You two hang back," Mr. Thompson called out after the bell rang. Nova and I looked at each other and stayed seated. After all the other students left, he stood in the aisle between our desks. "I know this is your first offence, Miss Mavros," he said, first turning to me. "But I intend to make an example out of you."

"Yes, sir," I croaked. "I understand." I was hardly ever in trouble like this.

"As for you, Nova," he said, turning his attention to her, "we will become even better friends now that this will be the . . . fifth time you will be joining my detention group this year."

Nova was looking down, but I caught her roll her eyes.

"Next time you will be suspended." He seemed to be taking delight in the thought he had Nova scared, but she looked utterly bored with his threat and continued to roll her eyes.

"What a fucking prick!" Nova said a little too loud as we left the class. "As if I don't have anything better to do during lunch. Well, at least you'll be there too, which I'm sorry about."

"You're such a bad influence, Nova. It was bound to happen," I joked.

We both laughed and I hurried off to math class while Nova veered off to geography.

Math class dragged on. It was overly boring, and I just wrote down the problems and decided to figure them out with a calculator later.

Detention on the other hand wasn't so bad. Nova and I just texted each other the whole time. The school was pretty relaxed about phones in school as long as they were off in class; in detention, nobody cared.

In art, I worked on my sketch and for the free period, I just waited around.

I saw Lucas after school waiting by his truck. I thought about going to talk to him, but I didn't want Nova or the other girls seeing me. I just waited far enough away, so hopefully, he wouldn't notice me.

Yia Yia picked me up from school and we got premade salads for dinner on the way home. I decided I wasn't going to tell her about my detention. Hopefully, it wouldn't happen again. If it did, I was almost certain the school would call her, but I would cross that bridge when I came to it.

Thursday dragged on in anticipation of the party, but finally, the day rolled around. Lucas was extra creepy whenever I saw him. He was always staring at me when he thought I wasn't looking. At lunch, Sythera, Nova, Nikki, Jill and I worked on the playlist for the party. This weekend couldn't come soon enough.

Friday, June 25

"I'm so excited for tomorrow!" Nova exclaimed on the way home.

"Me too. What time were you thinking of picking me up?" I asked.

"I'll come get you at six o'clock. The party starts at nine, so that will give us plenty of time to do our makeup, get dressed and drink. We'll be just the right kind of drunk when the party starts."

I wasn't sure about the drinking, but I pushed it to the back of my mind. No use in worrying about that now.

That night I watched a movie with Yia Yia and Shade. Shade spent the whole time kneading her favourite blanket that was draped over me. I went to bed later than expected. Yia Yia knew I was sleeping over at Sythera's the next day, so she let me sleep in until eleven.

CHAPTER

Saturday, June 26

I showered and impatiently watched the clock. I was SO excited. I said goodbye to Yia Yia and Shade when I saw Nova pull up, and I was off.

On the way to the party, Nova asked me about Knox. I told her what the plan was, and she said she would help. This party was going to be great!

When we got to Sythera's we parked in the usual spot and had to wade through a parade of caterers, florists, waiters and men carrying DJ equipment.

Upstairs in Sythera's room, the girls were sitting on the bed again listening to music. It was still about five hours until the party, so we had lots of time to just relax.

"Hey, girls. We were just talking about Ivy's date," Nova informed them as we came in.

"I knew Knox would step up!" Sythera gushed, climbing off the bed and coming over to me. She literally started bouncing. "Oh, he's so cute! Good for you," she winked.

"So, Nikki," Nova asked, "who did you end up inviting tonight?"

"I forget his name. I'll point him out when he gets here," she said nonchalantly.

Sythera and Jill rolled their eyes. I guessed that was normal for her.

"Are you and Bro cool for now?" Nova asked Jill. It was so unclear if they were fighting again or not since Jill never seemed too worried about it.

"For now," Jill assured us.

We didn't have to ask Sythera; we already knew Marcus would be her date. And we knew Jason would be with Nova.

There was a faint knock on the door. Sythera's maid, Collette, poked her head in.

"What is it?" Sythera asked, exasperated.

"DJ wants to know where you like him to set up and caterer wants to know if you want glass or silver serving trays," Collette read from a little notepad.

"Collette you could honestly figure this out yourself. Stop interrupting us! These are the last questions I'm answering. In the lobby along the far wall and silver of course."

Collette bowed and hurried off.

"It's so hard to find good help," Sythera said, stretching out.

My phone beeped. I had a text from Yia Yia: Turn on the news. It's urgent!

"Sythera, can I turn on the news? My yia yia wants me to see something."

Sythera grabbed the remote and switched to the local news station. Chloe's image flashed on the screen. My heart stopped.

I ran over to the screen to hear better.

This is Sarah Borrows with an update on Chloe Ladas's disappearance case. Since finding her remains, countless tests and an extensive autopsy have been performed. New sources tell us that authorities believe scratches and bite wounds found on the victim's body could be the result of an attack by a mountain lion, which are known to hunt in this area. Still unexplained is who buried her body. Mountain lions are known to cover their kill with leaves or some other foliage but not to dig a hole and then re-cover it. The search for more clues has been expanded and investigators are now combing the surrounding area as mountain lions are also known to drag their prey from their prior attack site. We will update this story as more details are released. I'm Sarah Borrows with ATTV news.

I sat back feeling sick to my stomach. Attacked by an animal didn't make sense because she was buried. Maybe someone found her and buried her and didn't say anything because they didn't want to be a suspect or get involved, but that seemed unlikely. It also seemed like the only answer unless it wasn't a mountain lion.

"Ivy?" Nova said, sitting down on the couch beside me.

"She was a friend of mine," I said, gesturing to the screen.

Nova looked up just as another picture flashed across the screen.

"Oh . . . I'm sorry for your loss," she said putting an arm around me. I leaned into her and clutched her arm.

My chest stung and felt like it was going to collapse. My eyes tingled with tears, but I refused to let them fall which made my nose run. I grabbed a tissue from the box on the coffee table in front of us and tried to dab away the tears before they made it out of my eyes. I looked up at Nova, my lip trembling.

"Thank you," I said, my voice cracking. We wrapped each other in a caring hug and stayed that way until Sythera noticed.

"Everything OK?" she called.

"Ivy was really good friends with Chloe Ladas," Nova said, gesturing to the TV.

All the girls came over to sit beside me.

Sythera watched for a moment and then reached her arm around me. "That poor, poor girl," Sythera sighed.

"Did you know her?" I asked teary-eyed.

"Not very well, but I remember her being a very sweet girl," Sythera recalled.

"It's a tragedy," Nikki said, jumping in.

"Very sad," Jill said, a hint of boredom in her voice.

Nova shot her an annoyed look and Jill shrunk back.

"Are you going to be OK?" Nikki asked.

"Yeah, I just need a minute," I said, getting up.

I walked to the ensuite in the far corner and closed the door.

I leaned over the sink. I had that sick feeling again. The image of Chloe being viciously ripped apart by a mountain lion while still alive was all I could think about over and over again. I started to shake and tried to think of something else, anything else. My mind drifted to Lucas. His touch warming my body. His eyes so caring and sincere. Then I remembered him leading me on and all feelings of sadness left my body, A new sensation of anger poured into the empty space. I slammed my fist down on the tile of the vanity. How stupid I was to think about him when I should have been thinking of Chloe. My temporary memory of him had replaced and erased the scenes of horror and with them gone, I was able to pull myself together. I took a deep breath and rinsed my face with cold water. I could do this. I was going to get through this, and all questions would be answered eventually. I just needed to be patient.

I didn't want to dampen the party and be gloomy the whole time, so I went back in, sat on the bed and just listened to the conversation that had sprouted about makeup options. I would have time to think about Chloe and everything else later. I texted Yia Yia that I had heard, made sure she was OK and said I would talk to her later. She said she was OK and urged me to try and have fun tonight.

About an hour passed when I was snapped out of my daze by a sudden rush of music from downstairs. The DJ had started playing.

"Time to get ready!" Nikki squealed.

Sythera ordered Collette to bring us some champagne. I very rarely drank when I lived with Sharron, since I had no friends and wasn't invited to many parties. But as long as Yia Yia didn't find out, I didn't see a problem with having a few drinks.

All the girls jumped off the bed and went to get dressed.

Sythera's costume was movie quality. Every detail was flawless. She had the hat, the black leather jacket with a nude tube top on under it and bright pink bikini bottoms on under her skin-tight black leather chaps. She finished the look with black studded fingerless gloves and matching bright pink high heels.

Jill had bought a reflector vest with a white tank top, tight jean shorts, a pink hard hat and a toy tool belt. She wore it all with high lace-up work boots.

Nikki had obviously been to a costume store and bought a one-piece police uniform. It was low cut at the top and the shorts came up incredibly high hugging her upper thighs. A belt with a toy gun, walkie talkie and badge hung loosely around her waist and her police hat fit perfectly along with her aviator sunglasses. Black leather knee-high skin-tight boots brought the whole outfit together.

Nova put on the cow print skirt and shirt she had picked out the other day. She tied the bottom of the shirt up in a knot to show off her midriff and the boots and hat she said she had looked great. She topped it off with a blue bandana that she tied around her neck and braided her hair into pigtails.

Lastly, I got dressed into my camouflage-print shorts and a black tank top. I completed the look by tying my hair in a loose braid, donning the hat, and putting on some simple black work boots.

We were ready for makeup.

Sythera filled up our glasses again.

Nova, Jill and Nikki all had relatively simple makeup. Sythera and I took ours a step further. She drew two thick lines on each cheek in red and I did the same in black.

We polished off the bottle of champagne and Collette rushed off to get some more before we headed downstairs.

We were ready.

CHAPTER 15

People had started to arrive by the time we got to the top of the stairs and everyone was either mingling or flocking from the kitchen with food and fancy-looking drinks. With our filled drinks in hand, we started down the stairs.

Nova spotted who I guessed must be Jason dressed up as a cowboy and ran to him. They obviously planned the couples costume. They looked great. They disappeared into the den as the other girls and I looked for our dates.

We made our way to the dance floor. "We will meet back here once we find our dates," Sythera shouted over the music. We all nodded and split up.

I knew I'd have an especially hard time finding Knox as I didn't know what he was dressed up as. I ventured into the kitchen.

"That's a pretty boring costume," said someone behind me. I turned to see the cheer squad—Joy, Brittney and Brandy.

"Excuse me?" I shot back.

"You have no imagination!" Brandy said, obviously unaware that her costume had been done a billion times over. None of their costumes required any thought. They were Scary, Ginger and Baby Spice of the Spice Girls.

"Where's Sporty and Posh?" I retorted. "Talk about unoriginal. By the way, I'm part of a group costume. Go find Sythera, Nova, Jill and Nikki. See if you have the intellectual capacity to figure it out; or am I using too many big words?"

Joy's eyes went wild. "Bitch!" she snorted and walked off with Brandy and Brittney close behind.

OK, that was rude. That wasn't my usual reaction to confrontation. Maybe the rage I had felt about Chloe's case hadn't completely subsided. I thought about apologizing, but I wanted to find Knox first. I filled my glass and lingered around the sour candy bowl while I thought about who Knox could be dressed as.

"May I have your attention, please," I heard Sythera say into a microphone. I stepped out of the kitchen along with everyone else to see her standing halfway up the staircase with the girls beside her. When she saw me, she smiled and waved me up. I hurried to her side and felt slightly off-balance with all the guests looking up at us.

"How amazing is it that this is the last weekend before school ends!" Sythera sang.

Everyone started to clap and cheer.

"That is what this party is for. Also, for those of you who don't know, this is my newest friend, Ivy, so it's almost kind of like a welcome party too." She put her arm around me. I could feel my face get hot. I just smiled like my legs didn't feel like jelly.

"Now, let's all get drunk!" Nikki yelled into the microphone.

Everyone cheered again. The music started back up and the caterers brought out more food.

Sythera pushed Nikki away once everyone turned to go back to dancing or talking. She looked furious that Nikki had stolen her thunder but regained her composure quickly as always.

Everyone else made their way to the dance floor, but I wanted to see if I could find Knox. Still no luck. "Is he standing me up?" I wondered.

I danced over to my group and saw Nova with Jason, Sythera with Marcus, dressed as a gladiator, Jill with Bro as a gangster and Nikki with some unknown guy dressed as a convict. He looked older, and knowing Nikki, he probably was. They were all dancing already.

"Ivy! This's Nate! He's in college!" she shouted and slurred over the music. I just smiled and gave a little wave.

"Where is Knox?" Nova asked as she kept dancing with her back to Jason.

I shrugged. "I haven't found him yet," I answered just as someone came up behind me and grabbed my hips.

"Let's dance," he said from behind me.

I tried to look behind me, but he seemed to dodge my view.

I assumed it was Knox, but then I saw Knox across the room dressed as some weird anime-looking knight. I spun around to see that a guy in a terrifying werewolf mask was my want-to-be dance partner. I stifled a shriek and took a step back.

Nova came over and grabbed my arm pulling me away from him. She practically hissed at him and Jason stepped between us. His muscles were especially visible due to him being topless and he had no problem flexing in his defensive stance. The guy stared him down for a few seconds, then finally turned and walked back to the kitchen.

"You OK, Ivy?" Jason asked, putting a hand on my shoulder.

I nodded. "Just a little startled."

"Want another drink?" he asked, taking my glass.

"Sure, thanks."

A shiver ran through me. "That werewolf guy better never show his ugly face near me again," I muttered to myself. "He needs to learn to keep his paws to himself."

I tried to forget him as I waved Knox over.

"Ye fun me. Ye keek stoatin," he mused.

We started to dance, but after a while my feet started hurting so I excused myself to take a breather. I found a chaise lounge set up in a little sitting area near the far wall. There, I had my glass filled up again by one of the skeleton-looking waiters that seemed unaware that no one here was old enough to be drinking legally. I decided they must have been getting paid a lot to overlook that little law. I settled down and looked around at all the costumed party-goers. There were pirates, movie characters, over-the-top celebrities alive and dead, superheroes and about a dozen girls dressed as cats, rabbits and angels. A group of girls were sitting next to me but took no notice. They were all drinking and laughing loudly, obviously drunk.

"Did you hear that girl Chloe was attacked by an animal?" one of the girls dressed as a unicorn spat out.

"I don't believe it. She was murdered by someone. Everyone knows that." A fairy speculated.

"Oh, you mean 'cause you killed her," a princess said jokingly.

"She was such a little snoop. She always acted so high and mighty like she knew everything," a sober deer said, squeezing between the fairy and unicorn.

I was about to come to Chloe's defence when I noticed the guy in the werewolf mask talking with another guy dressed up as the Flash with his back to me. Feeling rather brave—probably because of the amount of champagne I had drunk—I was going to approach him and ask him what his problem was.

"Hey!" I shouted walking up to him. He looked at me and then the other guy turned to look too. I stopped short. It was Lucas.

"What are you doing here? I'm quite sure you weren't invited," I said harshly.

"Whoa . . . have you been drinking? You smell like the back of a cheap limo," Lucas sneered.

"Go to hell, you bastard!" A few people looked at us, but I didn't care. How dare he insult me. He had no right to even be here.

"Calm down, I was joking," he said.

"No one here would have invited you, so leave!" I growled through gritted teeth. "Or I'll have Marcus throw you out!"

"I told you, I feel the irresistible urge to protect you so regardless of your feelings of hate toward me, I'm still going to watch out for you," Lucas said confidently. It was clear he wasn't going anywhere.

"You're the one who pushed me away! I mean it Lucas, stay away from me and tell your creepy friend to keep his hands to himself!" I said, glaring at the wolfman.

His friend then pulled his mask off. The wolfman had a short red mohawk and a tongue piercing. He was tall and handsome but that didn't matter. He was still a creep. "I can hear you," he said with a grin.

I walked off. I wanted nothing more to do with either of them. Sitting back down my head started to feel foggy. The adrenaline of talking to Lucas and the mention of Chloe was hitting me all at once. I felt flushed and I probably looked it too. Those girls seemed to have the same idea as me … that Chloe was murdered. The question was who killed her and why. I mean they obviously hadn't thought that highly of her, but they definitely didn't hate her enough to kill her.

A song that I liked came on, so I went to find Knox. Still in the same place I had left him, he was dancing with everyone else. The more I was around him the more I liked him. He was funny, a great dancer and every time he whispered in my ear with that sexy accent, I got shivers. He came to stand behind me and caressed my hips as I swayed to the music. I looked around at the other girls. It was pretty much the same with all the other couples in our group except Sythera and Marcus. They were facing each other with their foreheads touching. Marcus's arm was wrapped around Sythera's waist so tightly that it looked like she would have to struggle to move. It was almost like they were trying to meld into each other.

CHAPTER

16

As the night went on, partygoers started to leave the dance floor. Nova disappeared into a darkened den-like room with Jason, and soon after, Sythera and Marcus headed upstairs. All that was left from our group were Jill, Bro, Nikki, Nate, Knox and me. Bro left to get more beer and Jill followed. Nikki and Nate then went upstairs. There were more than a few dateless and overly drunk party guests still dancing and Knox and me.

My head was swimming, and I was starting to lose my balance.

"Wantae tak' a break sexy?" Knox asked, taking my hand.

I nodded and we headed upstairs. Seeing that most rooms were occupied, we made our way to Sythera's room, which surprisingly was empty.

"Ah lik' th' keek o' that kip," Knox said, pulling me toward him.

I filled my glass with the remaining champagne that Collette had brought up. The music was still pounding downstairs, but it was a little more muffled than other places in the house.

Knox had been drinking too and as we swayed, still slightly dancing to what we could hear, he pulled me even closer and softly kissed my forehead, then my eyelids, then he worked his way down to my mouth. I kissed him back; it felt nice and I wanted it!

Nikki and Nova burst through the door and stopped short. They both giggled.

"Sorry to interrupt," they said, "but we need to borrow Ivy."

"A' richt. Ah will juist hauld yer horses ower oan th' kip," Knox said, winking at me as he sat down on the bed.

Nova and Nikki pulled me down the hall into a vacant spare room.

"Jill just caught Bro with three other girls in a room just down the hall," Nova explained. "She's furious, but we aren't sure if we should tell Sythera. We are sure they are right in the middle of 'it.' What do you think we should do?"

That was an impossible question. I didn't even know what day it was anymore. I shrugged. "I don't know," I slurred.

They both looked at each other and pulled me to the room Sythera and Marcus were in. It was easy to find as the beaded necklace from Sythera's costume was hanging from the doorknob. Nikki knocked and heard "Go away!" from the other side of the door.

"It's Nikki. We have a problem."

"Oh for . . ." Sythera cracked the door open. "WHAT!"

"Jill caught Bro cheating on her with three other girls. She's really upset. What should we do?"

Sythera's expression changed from annoyance to pure rage. "Get dressed," she said over her shoulder. "I'll be right there," she said to us, closing the door.

A second later, Nova and Nikki were leading Sythera, Marcus and me to the room Bro and the three girls were in. Sythera kicked open the door and flicked on the lights. Bro fell off the bed, startled, as two girls screamed and covered up. Another girl, wearing only a skirt and Bro's gangster hat, fell off the other side of the bed. Bro was smashed; his pants were still on but undone. Marcus went in and grabbed Bro off the floor by the scruff of the neck and escorted him out the front door in front of everyone. Bro scrambled to pull his pants up. His expression was of pure terror.

"Go home!" Marcus yelled after him, closing the door.

"Where is Jill?" Sythera asked, turning to Nova, Nikki and me in almost a panic.

They pointed to the bathroom across the hall.

"I'll go check on her," Sythera said, walking toward the bathroom. "You guys go back to the party or whatever."

"Can I sleep in your room?" I asked, just in case she planned to sleep in there after she was done with Marcus.

"Yeah, sure. I'm going stay with Marcus," she said, smiling.

I mumbled a thank you and stumbled back to her room.

Knox was sitting on Sythera's bed sipping his beer. In an effort to make him laugh to lighten my mood, I did a bouncy dance over to him. I picked my glass up off the side table and continued to dance in front of him. He stood up and grabbed my waist and matched my swaying. He smelled so good, so I rested my head on his chest and closed my eyes.

I could feel him breathe me in and his arms moved up my back. He pulled the rest of my body closer with his strong embrace. I tilted my head up to look at him just as a new sultry song came on. He smiled down at me and after a while we resumed kissing. He sat down again, and I sat beside him. It just escalated from there. He pulled off his shirt as did I, and I kissed him again. He ran his hands down my braid and took out the hair tie. I shook my head and my hair fell around my shoulders. He loosely grabbed a strand and twisted it in his fingers as he kissed my neck. Sythera's silk sheets felt amazing on my bare skin. Before long, my eyes started to get heavy and I remember Knox rolling off me, but after that, nothing.

CHAPTER

17

Sunday, June 27

The next morning, I woke up with a pounding headache. A strip of sunlight snuck in and was shining right in my eyes. I turned to shield them. Once my vision came back, I realized Knox was beside me with his arm around my waist.

"Oh my god," I thought. "Please, tell me I didn't sleep with him." I checked to see if we were both wearing pants, and luckily, we were. I slid out from beneath Knox's arm and stumbled around the room to find my bra and top. Once I found them and got dressed, I steadied myself against the wall and made my way down the hall and stairs to the kitchen. People were passed out all over the place. Collette was running around trying to wake people, but no one seemed to pay her any attention. She looked up from a passed-out Joy and Brandy, who somehow ended up on top of the kitchen counter, when I walked in.

"Excuse me, Collette, but do you have aspirin and water?"

Collette looked at me like she had no idea what I was talking about. English wasn't her first language, but she seemed to understand Sythera just fine.

She walked up to a fridge filled with Gatorade and pointed at it with an eyebrow raised.

"Better than nothing," I thought.

I took enough for all the girls, their dates, Knox and me. I thought since I was the first one up it was the proper thing to do.

I first found Nova and Jason in a sitting room asleep on a couch together and left two bottles with them. Next, in the bedroom adjacent to the one Sythera and Marcus had stayed in, I found Nikki between Nate and another guy I hadn't seen before. I left two bottles for them. They obviously had no problem sharing.

I tiptoed into Sythera and Marcus's room and left their bottles on the side table. They were in bed together, Sythera's head resting on Marcus's chest, their costumes in untidy heaps on the floor.

Lastly, I found Jill still in the bathroom. She had passed out in the empty bathtub. Her face was streaked with tears and her makeup was smeared. She had evidently been crying all night; I felt so bad for her. Rather than wake her up and get into an awkward, hangover conversation, I left the Gatorade with her and slipped back out.

"Knox, wake up," I whispered, creeping back into Sythera's bedroom. He rolled over and opened one eye. A look of confusion and shock flickered over his face. He sat bolt upright.

"Whaur am ah?" he said, rubbing his forehead.

"In Sythera's room. Do you remember the party last night?" I asked.

"O' coorse, bit ah dinnae mind falling asleep in 'ere," he said, bewildered.

"Who knows when he blacked out?" I thought. "I guess he doesn't remember making out either."

After handing him the Gatorade I walked over to Sythera's vanity to check my hair and makeup. My hair was intact for the most part since it was down, but my makeup was a mess. The two thick black lines I had on my cheeks were smeared down to my jawbone and my eyeliner was smudged. I decided to clean it up a bit with some makeup remover. As I searched the vanity for a makeup wipe, I saw Knox get up and put on his shirt.

"Im aff tae gang noo. Cheers fur a fin night," he said when I turned around.

"Are you OK? You seem confused." He looked like he had done something wrong.

"A'm sae sorry a dinnae mind bit, did we . . . ye ken . . . bang?" he stumbled.

"I don't think so. We both had our pants on so . . ."

His expression changed and he looked a little more relaxed. He gave me a kiss and then left.

Later that day when the girls had woken up and all the stragglers had left, Jason and Nova drove me home.

I waved them off and tried to figure out how I was going to get past Yia Yia without her finding out about my hangover.

I found her in the den, and I did my best to just wave a hello and shuffle upstairs without letting her get a good look at me.

I collapsed onto my bed; it felt like my insides were on fire. My feet ached and my head pounded. Any movement made me helplessly dizzy. I tugged my purple curtains closed over the sheer ones in hopes of snuffing out any light. Shade jumped on me and nudged my face.

A knock at my door made me break into a cold sweat.

"Ivy?" Yia Yia called. She walked in before I had time to even lift my head.

"I thought so . . . well I can't say I approve since you're only sixteen, but I think you're being punished enough for now," she said, shaking her head.

I honestly felt ashamed.

"You know it's going to be difficult to trust you now. Please don't make me go through raising your mother again."

"I'm sorry, Yia Yia. I can honestly tell you I'm not going to drink again until I'm of age and maybe not even then. This is the worst I've felt in . . . a really long time," I said, covering my eyes.

"Well, you need to eat. Dinner will be ready in a couple of hours; I expect you to join me," she said and closed my door.

"That went better than I could have hoped," I thought. "I can spend the rest of the day in my room, and all I have to do is join her for dinner. Hopefully, we can move on after that."

CHAPTER

18

Monday, June 28

By the time Monday rolled around, Yia Yia had lightened up about my mistake and things were a little more relaxed. The only things that changed were I had to tell her where I was going, text her who I was with, when I was going to be back, and I wasn't allowed to stay the night anywhere; I now had a curfew until she felt she could trust me. I thought that was fair and accepted it. I knew it could be way worse, and I probably deserved it, but I was glad she was reasonable.

The only other time I had gotten drunk and had a hangover, Sharron never found out. If she had, she probably would have locked me away. Any excuse to keep me under her thumb.

I hadn't talked to Lucas since the night of the party; it had me on edge. Had he listened to me and given up trying to contact me or was he just trying to make me sweat? I didn't care either way. I was kind of into Knox, but so was every other girl who heard him speak. I wasn't sure I was ready to fight for any guy now. I was fine being single.

The whole conundrum made my head hurt. I was sitting in the den by the window with Shade when Shade suddenly jerked her head like she was alerted by something. It made me look in the same direction. She was intently looking at Chloe's house, which was slightly obscured by the bushes that divided Yia Yia and the Ladas's property. Maybe it was my want or need to talk to someone. I had an hour before school started and Yia Yia was out, so I sprinted over to Chloe's house. I had put this off long enough. I crept around to the side opposite Yia Yia's house and broke open the back door leading to the kitchen.

The floor was covered in dried leaves, broken boards, glass and dead bugs. "Why didn't I bring my can of spider killer?" They had left their kitchen table behind, and a coffee maker still sat on the counter in the corner next to the door. Walking carefully, so as not to disturb anything—or alert any spiders—I started to look around. I could picture where everything used to be. It was so eerie to see it so empty and dilapidated.

Moving to the living room at the front of the house, I remembered playing hide-and-seek in there. I recalled the best place to hide was behind her dad's reading chair, which used to be in the corner next to the gigantic bookshelf. Everything was gone now. The room seemed way too big and in no way cozy like it was before.

I slowly climbed the staircase, watching that I didn't step on any loose boards, and stepped over pieces of glass from a mirror that looked like it had been left behind and had fallen off the wall at some point. The first bedroom upstairs was

Chloe's parents' room, which was empty and surprisingly clean except for the broken windows. The bathroom was across the hall and Chloe's room was next to it.

I gently pushed open the door to her room. Broken wood and shingles littered the floor from where the storm had ripped open the roof. The warm sun beat down on the wooden bed frame and dresser against the wall. Sliding boards and garbage out of the way with my foot, I cleared a path to the dresser. With reluctance, thinking I would find a rat nest or a thriving bug colony, I opened each of the drawers. A few messy, dust-covered pieces of paper were left in the first drawer. Nothing was in any of the others. Just I was about to close the top drawer, I remembered something. The bottom drawer had a false bottom that only Chloe and I knew about. Only a specific set of knocks and slight jiggles would make it open, and because I had done it with Chloe many times in the past, I knew just how to pop it open. Three hard knocks on the side of the drawer, push hard on the top and jiggle to the left slightly. It burst open, spraying dust everywhere. I waved the air trying to push the dust away from my face. When my eyes refocused, my memory was submerged into the eerie past. There was a friendship bracelet I had made her in third grade, a picture of us at the beach and a few other little things, like bubble gum and our stories about Greek myths all laid out carefully. I searched around trying not to disturb too much until I felt something soft. I reached beneath the thick layer of dust and pulled out a pink notebook with a broken lock on the front. "Chloe's Journal" was written in gold loopy letters on the cover. Opening to the first page, I read:

Stakeout

Day 12:

These girls are not human; I'm almost certain. I've been watching them more closely lately and they always seem to go to her house. I never see them leave. They can't all live there alone. And their boyfriends, the only normal one is the guy with the goth-looking girl. There is something sinister about the other two guys though. They act like they have lived here forever but I've never seen them before. The only upside is the cute guy that showed up a few weeks after them. Lucas, I think his name is, is unbelievably cute. I bet Ivy would like him. He's definitely her type. I hope this summer she gets a chance to meet him.

I scanned the page looking for a date but there wasn't one. The heading said, "Day 12." "Why does it start there?" I wondered. "Is there another book with the previous days?" I looked around for other pages but couldn't find anything. I flipped through the pages and a folded paper tucked between two blank pages fell to the floor. I picked it up and unfolded it. I recognized it immediately. It was my myth. She had kept my copy.

I started to feel the tears as I ran my hand over the writing, but then I heard a creak from behind me in the hallway and turned to see a shadow duck from view. I froze. The shadow was still watching me. I could feel it.

Trembling, I tucked the book under my arm and shakily took a few steps toward the door. I had to find out who it was. I suddenly had a rush of adrenaline and shot forward shoving the door open wildly. The shadow moved just in time for me to see it running down the stairs as I crashed into the hallway. I got to the top of the stairs leading to the foyer just as a board that had been nailed to the frame to keep people from breaking in was torn and thrown off the front door. It landed on the step infront of me. The light from the now open front door blinded me while whatever it was ran out. Stumbling down the stairs, I ran out after it, but it had vanished.

That day at school, Nova ran into our English class before Mr. Thompson got there and pulled me out to the nearest girls' bathroom. All the other girls were waiting there.

"He has to pay!" I heard Sythera declare as we entered. "Ivy," she said, welcoming us. "I'm sure you remember what Bro did to Jill at my party."

"That fucking troll!" Nikki sneered.

Jill was quiet; eerily quiet. It was like the only emotion left in her was rage and that if someone said the wrong thing, she would go absolutely insane. I shuttered; I didn't want to be within a thousand miles of her when she finally broke down. She seemed like the type who would set fire to something important if she were angry.

"We need to make him pay," Sythera declared, whipping everyone but Jill into a frenzy.

"NO!" Jill suddenly snapped.

Everyone looked at her.

"But I thought—" Nikki started.

"I don't care what you thought, and I don't care what he did. He's nothing to me anymore, so let's just leave it at that. He will get his eventually; he was with three girls after all. Maybe I'll get lucky when karma catches up and he gets an STD or something."

Sythera smiled. "That would be perfect."

"So, you're fine?" Nova asked carefully.

"Yes. I mean I'm not happy, but I'll move on," Jill said, shrugging.

The bell rang so we all parted ways. Nova and I ran back to class just before Mr. Thompson closed the door.

"Sorry I pulled you out of class so fast before," Nova said later as we made our way to lunch. "From the way Jill was talking, I thought we were going to plan revenge against Bro. She was adamant about making him pay, but in the time I left to get you she must have changed her mind. She's very sneaky though. She's probably planned something but just doesn't want anyone else to be part of it. Knowing her, she is probably going to do something 'earth-shattering' to him like 'notify his parents,' " she said using air quotes around "earth-shattering" and "notify his parents." "By the way," she continued, "what happened with you and Knox?"

"I'm glad you came and got me, Nova. I was really worried about Jill, but I think it was very mature of her not to want to stir the pot and possibly make things worse. I mean, I can understand the thought of revenge, but it really wouldn't help anything. Let's hope she really has let it go. As for Knox, I'm not sure what we are. I like him . . . a lot … but I'm not sure I'm ready for a boyfriend.

"Well, you could just be friends with benefits until you're ready to date."

"No, I'm not going to be greedy. I'm totally fine just being regular friends with him."

"Well, now is your chance to tell him," she said, pointing down the hall.

I turned to see Knox was walking toward us.

"I'll see you at our normal spot," she said, hurrying off.

"Awright sexy. Syther's pairtie wis fin," Knox said, giving me a kiss on the cheek.

"Yeah, I had fun too. Listen, I really like you, but I think we would be better as just friends."

His smile faded. "Och. Weel ah jalouse thats a'richt. Ah wis hoping we cuid mibbie date bit ah ken."

"I'm sorry, Knox. I hope we can be friends?" I felt so bad that I upset him, but I didn't want to lead him on.

"Tis a'richt. Ah will see ye around," he said, his smile returning, though a bit forced now. He kissed my forehead and headed off to his next class.

I felt horrible. I wish it had never gotten so serious at Sythera's party, but at least I didn't sleep with him. That would have been a billion times worse.

I found the girls at our usual spot by the statue. Sythera was talking to Marcus in hushed tones near the back of the statue close to the tip of the Chimera's snake tail, and Nikki was talking to Jill on the other side beside the Chimera's left paw. Jason was nuzzling Nova's neck. She whispered something and he grabbed her up in his arms and hugged her tightly, kissing her hair.

Suddenly Bro rounded the corner into the hall. Jill's face went beet red and she started to shake with fury. Bro stopped several feet away knowing he probably shouldn't get too close.

"Jill, baby can we talk?" he asked.

"Not on your life!" Nikki growled.

Sythera and Marcus halted their conversation.

"How dare you show your fucking face here after what you did!" Sythera screamed.

Marcus held her back as she started to charge.

Bro backed up a little. "I just wanted to tell you I've been called home," he said, holding up his hands in defence.

Sythera stopped and looked at Marcus in terror. Nikki, Nova and Jill all looked at Sythera.

"My father is terribly angry with me after he heard what happened, so I'm being sent back home. I'm so sorry Jill. I love you."

I looked at Jill. She really had told his parents. I felt sorry for Bro; he really did sound sincere, but I didn't know much about their relationship before this so maybe he always sounded that way.

Jill's face was still red but now fear replaced anger. After Bro was out of sight, Sythera spoke. "Ummm . . . *orepei nha milisoume*," she said in Greek, her voice trembling.

Everyone except Jason and I nodded vigorously.

"I'm sorry, Ivy," Sythera said sweetly, as everyone's gaze turned to Jason and me. "I know we are friends, but this is something incredibly sensitive … and you wouldn't understand what we are talking about anyways. This situation goes back way before we met you. Could you both give us a few minutes?"

"Bye, honey," Nova said, blowing Jason a kiss. Turning to me she said, "I'll drive you home after school, Ivy."

"Oh, uh OK. See you guys later," I stammered. It was awkward, but I supposed everyone had some things they wanted to keep private.

"They always tend to do that," Jason said, noticing my puzzlement. "Don't take it personally. It's probably due to their upbringing."

I wondered what he meant by that, but he saw some friends and ran off to join them, leaving me in a frozen state of confusion.

When I saw Nova again after school, her face was full of worry. She was usually talkative and cheerful on the drive home, but this time she kept chewing her lip and had a white-knuckle grip on the steering wheel.

I wanted to ask her if she was OK. I knew something about what Bro had said spooked her, and I knew Sythera and the others were hiding something. I suspected that even if I asked, she wouldn't tell me, so I kept quiet.

As I went to get out of the truck, Nova grabbed my wrist. "Wait, I forgot to give you something." She reached into her bag, pulled out a small velvet box and handed it to me. I raised an eyebrow. "Open it."

I slowly opened the box and was immediately taken aback. Inside was a small swan pendant on a delicate silver chain. "Oh, Nova! It's beautiful!" I exclaimed, putting on the necklace.

"The girls and I bought it for you. You're one of us," she said, finally smiling.

I smiled back. "Thank you." I hugged her almost wanting to cry with happiness. I finally felt like I belonged to something, that I had something I had never had anywhere else. Friends. Real friends!

"I'll see you tomorrow," I said, waving to Nova as she drove away.

CHAPTER

19

Up in my room, I was greeted by Shade winding herself around my legs. "What?" I asked her. Bending down I showed her the necklace Nova had given me. "Look, isn't it beautiful?"

Shade hissed and jumped onto my bed. Her fur was standing on end and her back was arched like something had scared her.

"What's your problem?" I questioned.

She hissed at me again, so I shooed her out of my room.

As she jumped off my bed, she knocked Chloe's journal off my nightstand. I picked it up and sat down to read some more.

Day 16

I had to sneak through the woods, but I finally got a good view of her house. It's been four days and I've documented when they leave and when they come back. It's the same time every day, so it will be easy to do some reconnaissance when they are not there. Her room is on the second storey, so I couldn't see anything from the yard. Next step is to gain evidence from inside.

I couldn't believe Chloe would go as far as to actually break into someone's house. She was serious about whatever this was.

Day 17

I've been trying to figure out if what I saw was actually real. I broke into her house after they all left for school, but the maid was still there. She was standing at the end of the staircase perfectly still. She didn't seem to see me and didn't respond to any movement or sound. It looked as if she was in a trance and though that was incredibly weird that wasn't the worst thing I saw.

Day 18

I searched the first floor and noticed there was no food whatsoever in the house. Next, I checked upstairs and all but four rooms were empty. The rooms that weren't empty looked like typical teenage girls' rooms except for the fact that they were immaculately tidy and organized. The beds looked like they had never been slept in. Because everything was strategically placed, I did my best not to disturb anything. I scanned the vanity, opened the ensuite cupboards, rifled through the closet and looked under the bed. Nothing was out of place until I noticed a red spot on the face of the bedside table drawer. I opened it and almost fainted. It was a finger. A severed finger! Not daring to touch it, I did my best to examine it from afar. It looked like it had been bitten off. Like an animal or something had torn off this person's finger and then spit it out. This was insane. If this girl was keeping a bloody rotting finger in her side table, there was definitely something wrong with them. I didn't have time to look in the basement before they were due home, so I slipped out the back door and ran back through the woods to my house. I'll have to go back later to check out the basement.

My breath caught in my chest. Was she crazy?! She couldn't go back in there. They had a friggin' body part in a drawer. I was just about to read the next page when I heard a vehicle pulling up. I looked out my window and saw it was Yia Yia. She was back from shopping. I ran down and opened the door to help her bring everything in. That's when I saw Lucas pulling his truck in behind her.

"Oh, good you're home. Lucas has been looking for you," Yia Yia beamed, walking in with her arms full of groceries.

I rolled my eyes. "Thanks."

"Can we talk . . . in private?" he asked, putting a few more bags of food down just inside the front door.

I waved him up to my room. "We are just going to discuss some schoolwork, Yia Yia," I called over my shoulder.

"OK, dinner will be ready soon. Lucas, would you like to stay for dinner?" she said sweetly.

"He can't," I answered for him and continued up to my room.

"Didn't I tell you to stay away from me?" I said, shoving Chloe's journal under my pillow and sitting on my bed.

"Didn't I tell you I couldn't!" he said, exasperated, closing my door.

"What did you want to talk about?" I said, changing the subject.

"Ivy, I don't want to stay away from you any longer. I've had time and I think I've come to terms with Daphne's death. My friend Rooster that you met at Sythera's party helped me through it. He's like a brother to me and somehow, he changed my way of thinking about what happened. I know now it wasn't completely my fault. I was a factor and in the wrong place at the wrong time. I did all I could. He also made me realize my true feelings for you. I know you slept with that Knox guy that night and it almost killed me."

"Oh, I needed to find myself, that's why I pushed you away, but now I want you back because you're so special to me and you're interested in someone else," I mocked. "You don't know anything. I never slept with Knox. All we did was make out and fall asleep in the same bed. Not that it's any of your business," I said defensively.

He sighed with relief and continued. "I know it sounds cliché, but it's true. I want to be with you, Ivy, and now . . . wait . . . where did you get that?" he said, reaching out to touch my necklace.

I wrapped my hand around the swan pendant and turned away from him. "From Nova. The girls bought it for me because I'm their friend."

"You actually believe that!? Are you insane!?" he screeched.

"What!?" I said, my rage building. I turned to face him. I wanted to strangle him.

He reached out and grabbed the necklace, ripping it off my neck.

"How dare you!" I screamed. I tried to grab it back, but he held it tightly in his fist.

"You have no idea how dangerous it is to ask me to leave. This proves it!" Lucas yelled threateningly. "Now they will know everything you do. This thing will help them control you!"

"No, what's dangerous is me having to deal with your emotional whiplash. You sound ridiculous! Do you hear yourself?! Give me my necklace and get OUT, you psycho."

"I love you, Ivy, and I want to be with you. I need to protect you!"

"But I don't love you!" I spat. But as soon as I said it, I regretted it. "Do I really not love him or am I just mad?" I wondered. I didn't believe that over one weekend he had figured his shit out. "No one can get over a death they believe they caused that quickly," I thought. "Still, he didn't really cause it. Maybe I'm so mad because I do love him but have given up trying to understand him? Maybe I'm just as messed up as him."

"Ivy, I wish you could see the real me, but of course you're too stubborn to give me a second chance. Those bitches you call friends have brainwashed you."

I held out my hand for him to give me back the necklace, but he threw it down and stepped on it, breaking the neck of the swan.

I stared in disbelief at what he had just done. "Leave now. I never want to see you again," I said numbly.

I heard him leave my room and shut the door behind him. I bent down and picked up the broken pieces of the necklace. Cradling the pieces in my hands, I gently set them down on my bedside table; maybe I could fix it. I started to tear up. It felt as if he had just killed a real swan. The pendant, a beautiful token of friendship, was now just a broken piece of metal shaped by jealously. I went to my window to watch Lucas drive away. I wanted to make sure he really was going to leave me and not look back.

How could he have done that? The girls—my friends—had given me a thoughtful gift, something that made me feel accepted and wanted. He knew how important that was to me.

I drew back my curtains and squinted through the sunset to see the truck speed onto the roadway. Just before he got to the downhill slope someone ran in front of his truck. He swerved to miss whoever it was, but he was going too fast. He violently lost control and slid straight into a power-line pole.

I watched in horror as the person turned to look at the damage she had caused. Her silhouette was traced out perfectly by the sun; it was the same silhouette I had seen that night in the town parking lot. It was probably also the shadow I had seen earlier in the day at Chloe's house. I strained to see who it was, but I couldn't get past the glare.

"Yia Yia, call 911!" I screamed as I ran out the door. I sprinted to Lucas's truck and ran to the driver's side to look in the window. The door was stuck but the window had been shattered. He seemed to be unconscious and was bleeding heavily from a gash on his forehead. He had several cuts on his face, arms and pretty much all his exposed skin.

"Lucas! Lucas! If you can hear me, hang on. Help is on its way. Just hold on," I said, calling through the window. He wasn't moving or responding to my voice. I wanted to check his pulse but was too shaken to touch him.

"They're coming, honey!" Yia Yia called from the porch, her voice wobbly.

I attempted to wrench the driver's side door open, but the frame was so bent that the door was stuck. Holding my breath and trying to see through my tears, I watched as each second passed painfully slowly, until finally, I saw his chest slightly rise and fall.

Suddenly, I heard a faint, eerie giggle behind me. A sharp shiver ran up my spine as I straightened and turned toward the sound. All I saw were two piercing green eyes. I stumbled backward, dizzily, and my temples started to throb. Bile rose in my throat and my heart started beating faster as I crumpled to the ground. My stomach twisted itself into a burning knot. "Am I having a panic attack?

Am I going into shock?" I wondered. I felt the blood drain from my face and the colour of the world suddenly fizzle to black.

I stared at the discoloured, dirt-smudged linoleum in the seemingly quiet hospital emergency waiting room. The town's hospital was very small but more than adequate for the population. I was still shivering and had a headache, but I had awoken briefly when the EMTs arrived at the scene. Seeing I was slightly awake and responsive, they immediately turned their attention to Lucas. I was glad. All I remembered before being lifted into a second ambulance was saying, "Save him," and looking over at the crumpled truck before passing out again.

CHAPTER

20

After a few hours at the hospital, I was cleared to go. The doctor explained that I was in shock and the trauma of what I saw probably was what caused me to faint. I started to feel better and asked to see Lucas. They told me he was in surgery and that his next of kin had the right to see him first. I wasn't leaving until he was out of surgery, so there I sat in the waiting room.

An old black-and-white TV popped and crackled in the corner of the room. Suddenly, I heard, "This is Sarah Borrows reporting. The remains of fifteen-year-old Chloe Ladas were found at a construction site near Black Creek fifteen days ago. There have been new developments in the case ruled as an animal attack. Police now believe she was brutally attacked by several suspects and the coroner has determined the cause of death to be from blunt force trauma to the head. Police urge anyone with information about this case or events leading up to this case to come forward. I'm Sarah Borrows ATTV news."

The TV reception was fuzzy, but I could make out the picture of Chloe clearly. I wondered if I should go to the police and tell them I knew Chloe, but since I had only seen her in the summer, I didn't know very much about her other friends, what she did during the rest of the year or her school life. I did have her journal, but I wanted to finish reading it before I gave it to them. This was all too much to think about, especially when Lucas could be dying on the operating table as I waited.

The minutes turned into an hour before the automatic door swung open, blasting air into the room. A girl in a bright blue tank top and black yoga pants sprinted to the reception desk.

"I'm Luna Teresi. My brother came in earlier. He was in a car accident?" she breathed.

"Ah yes, Miss Teresi. I have your brother's information here. Are your parents present?" the receptionist asked, looking over Luna's shoulder.

"Uh . . . no. We were raised by friends of my parents, but we live on our own now."

The receptionist looked skeptical but informed Luna of Lucas's current condition and asked her to have a seat. The second she turned, her eyes landed on me. It was almost as if she had sensed me there. I stiffened as she lunged at me.

"This is all your fault!" she growled.

I opened my mouth to defend myself, but what could I say? That it wasn't my fault? We both knew it was. I had made him angry which forced him to speed off the way he did. I fully blamed myself but hearing someone else say it made it seem more . . . real.

She walked to the far side of the room and sat down.

All I could do was hope Lucas was OK, pray that he would come out of surgery alive and have faith in his strength to pull through.

A few minutes later, I saw Rooster come through the emergency doors and scan the room. He found me first and started to walk toward me. A sharp whistle momentarily pierced the air, making me jump, and we both looked toward the sound. Luna was waving Rooster over.

He quickly looked back at me and walked over to sit with her. He hugged her and they started talking in hushed tones, so I returned my view to the floor and continued to pray.

"Miss Teresi," the receptionist called over the PA about an hour later. My head snapped up and Luna dashed to the desk. The receptionist pointed to the double doors to the right of the desk.

"Hello, my name is Dr. Soper. I operated on your brother," I heard a man with light silver hair explain to Luna near the door to the operating room. "The surgery was successful, and Lucas is now stable—"

"Can I see him?" Luna interrupted.

"Yes, but even though the surgery was a success he . . . he's in a coma."

I heard Luna gasp in unison with me. I slowly stood.

"I need to be with him. He's all I have," Luna said, a single tear running down her face.

I stared after them as Dr. Soper led her to Lucas's room. I wanted to run after them. I needed to see him, to apologize and tell him I really did love him. I wished I could take back what I had said.

"Come on," someone said behind me. "I'll take you home." It was Rooster.

"I'm not going anywhere. I have to see Lucas, and I'm not leaving until I do," I protested, planting my feet.

"There is no way you're going to see him tonight. I'll bring you back tomorrow if you'd like, but I think for now Luna should have her time alone with him."

I thought about that for a moment. She was his sister after all. His only family. I sighed deeply and nodded.

"OK, follow me," he said with his hand on my back.

CHAPTER

TUESDAY, JUNE 29

When Rooster and I pulled into Yia Yia's driveway, I could see her hurry from the couch in the den to the door. It was late but she had stayed up. She scurried to the car and helped me out. "Oh my gods, Ivy, I was so worried. Are you OK?" she cried, hugging me. "I'm so sorry I couldn't follow you to the hospital. The police kept me so long taking my statement and what not that by the time they were finished Rooster had called to tell me that you were OK and that he'd bring you home."

"They said I fainted from shock and overexertion. I'm OK," I assured her.

She hurried me inside and sat me on the couch in the den, wrapping a flannel blanket around me. "I'll make you some tea," she said and disappeared into the kitchen just as Rooster appeared in the entryway.

"You OK?" he asked, sitting down on the coffee table across from me.

I nodded. "I just hope Lucas is."

"He's a tough guy. If the past is any indication, he'll pull through this," he said, trying to restore my hope.

"He never mentioned you, which seems odd because of the history you apparently have together," I said, wondering why Lucas hadn't told me about his best friend.

"I've spent a few years . . . abroad. We've been best friends for a long time and the only person that knows him better than me is Luna. But she would rather die than talk to you right now," he joked.

I pulled my knees to my chest and hugged them tightly.

"Rooster," Yia Yia said, coming into the den with a tray of tea and *thaktila*. "Thank you for bringing Ivy home." She smiled setting the tray down and handing Rooster and me each a mug.

"You know him?" I asked her, surprised.

"Of course. He's Lucas's best friend. I've known him for a long time. Almost as long as I've known Lucas," she said, equally surprised that I didn't think of that. "How is he?" she asked her face creased with concern.

"He's stable but in a coma," Rooster explained. "Luna told me she is going to stay there until he wakes up . . . however long it takes."

"The poor thing. She must be so worried," Yia Yia said, shaking her head sadly. "Such a tragedy. It couldn't have happened to a nicer boy."

I nodded absentmindedly.

"I have to swing by their house and bring Luna a change of clothes. I can pick you up tomorrow, Ivy, if you want to go," Rooster said, setting down the mug of tea.

"Please," I answered, barely letting him finish.

He nodded and mimed a goodbye.

My previous opinion of Rooster had changed. He seemed genuinely concerned about Lucas and Luna. Yia Yia obviously knew him and trusted him. First impressions were usually wrong in my experience. I decided he was a really nice guy and only wanted to help. I didn't know much about him still, but for the time being, I was going to trust him and take the support he offered.

The next morning, I sat up feeling better until the image of Lucas's mangled body lying in his truck flooded my mind. I got dressed quickly and texted Rooster to tell him I was ready. Yia Yia had called the school already and told them what had happened and that I would be away for the day. I was too anxious to eat before I left. Yia Yia gave me a few premade meals to give to Luna.

When we got to the hospital Rooster showed me to Lucas's room. I took a deep breath before I walked in. I tried to mentally prepare myself for what might be waiting for me.

The dull blue light emanating from the medical equipment seemed to stamp out any chance of cheer that might be hiding in Lucas's small room. Luna was staring blankly out the window but glanced back when we entered. Her eyes seemed to focus and her body became rigid when she saw me.

"What the fuck is she doing here?" Luna squeezed out, rising weakly to her feet.

"Don't upset yourself further," Rooster said, holding up his hands as he approached her. "Let's talk in the hall. I'll explain," he said, gesturing for her to lead the way.

"I'm not leaving him with her," she said, eyeing me like I was death itself.

"He will be fine," Rooster said, continuing to coax her out of the room.

I was glued to the spot beside the door; her stare was shooting through me like a flaming arrow.

As Rooster closed the door behind them, I crept to the curtain surrounding the bed that was holding the broken body of someone I once knew. Lucas had been reduced to just a shell of who he had been just the previous day. His face was completely unrecognizable and his skin a sinister and unnatural rainbow of purple, brown, blood red and blue; it was heartbreaking to look at him. I tried to push the thought of how much pain he must be in out of my head. Could he feel any pain? I placed the meals on the windowsill I had brought for Luna and pulled the chair closer to the bed. I scanned his body for any sign that it really was him. The only indication was the barely visible tattoo of the sun on his shoulder peaking through the bruises like they were cloud cover.

"Lucas?" I whispered. "It's Ivy." I waited . . . I wasn't sure for what. I knew he wouldn't answer but I held onto a false hope that my voice would wake him up, like some magical power.

"Lucas, I'm sorry . . . this is all my fault. I didn't mean what I said. I was angry, and I'm sorry I didn't believe you. I . . . I do love you." I waited for another answer that wouldn't come.

I reached out and placed my hand on his. I waited to feel that heat, that warmth that always filled me whenever I touched him, but I didn't feel it. I felt nothing but cold cracked skin. I looked at his face and visualized what he normally looked like. How I remembered him was the day he picked me up for school when the sun was drenching him in such a brilliant light that he practically shone as we drove. I held onto that Lucas and stood leaning over him.

"I know you can hear me. Please, wake up," I whispered. "Please . . . please wake up." I searched his face for any hint of movement. Several seconds passed and nothing happened. I started to give up. I thought about leaving but something drew me to stay with him. With a shaking hand, I ran my fingers down his cheek and then to the side of his neck. Without even second-guessing it, I kissed his forehead very gently. "I love you," I said, again willing him to open his eyes.

"Get the fuck away from him!" Luna snarled, bursting back into the room. "You have no business being here, you murderer!" she hissed as she reached the foot of the bed. I slid my hand back from Lucas and backed away.

"There's some food my yia yia made for you here," I said, gesturing to the windowsill.

Her gaze never left me as I moved to stand with Rooster by the door.

"We will talk later," Rooster said to Luna. "Call me if anything changes and get some sleep."

Luna looked back at Lucas and went to sit in the chair, worry on her face replacing all the hatred directed at me.

CHAPTER

On the way home I asked, "Rooster, before the accident Lucas said it would be dangerous for me to send him away. . . . Do you know why?"

Rooster looked startled. "I'm not sure. . . . I shouldn't be telling you this, Ivy, but . . . you are in danger. They brainwashed you surprisingly well."

"What!? Who!?" I had a suspicion about who he was talking about, but I wanted him to say it.

"They aren't who you think they are. Sythera and the others are not your friends."

"You sound just like Lucas," I complained, crossing my arms.

"Then don't you think you should listen? Why would he lie? Why would I?"

"Because he's jealous. I have other friends and you're his friend, so of course you would agree with him."

"Oh, come on, Ivy. Don't flatter yourself," Rooster laughed, shaking his head.

"Fuck you! You know nothing about me. Lucas seems to think he needs to protect me ... like it's his duty or something. Explain that!"

"It's because of your father!"

I froze. "Wh . . . what did you just say?"

"Your father! Will—"

"How do you know about him?"

"Everyone does. Sythera, Nova, Nikki and Jill are working for him." In a gentler voice he added, "Your father is Hades, Ivy. He wants you in the underworld with him."

I didn't know what to say. Rooster had snapped. He honestly thought I would believe him. This was some kind of sick joke at the worst possible time. "You're psycho. You're completely insane!"

"I wish I were making this up, but I'm telling the truth. Why would I joke about this!?"

I bolted out of the car the second he pulled into Yia Yia's driveway.

"Ivy! Wait!" he shouted after me.

I ran to find Yia Yia. She was sitting at the kitchen table.

"What's wrong? Is it Lucas?" she asked when she saw my face.

"Rooster is scaring me! He's saying Hades is my father and that my friends are working for him. He's lost his mind."

"THEY ARE!" Rooster said, appearing in the doorway behind me.

"Back off!" I screamed, stepping between him and Yia Yia.

"Ivy, he's telling the truth," Yia Yia said, suddenly standing up. "Rooster is actually Hermes."

I slowly turned to face her. She looked dead serious. This couldn't be happening.

She then proceeded to tell me the same thing Rooster … Hermes? … had said except for the part about Sythera and the other girls. She didn't know about them, but then again, she had never met any of them.

I sat down slowly in a daze.

"Your mom has been trying to hide you since you were born," Yia Yia explained. "That's why you moved around so much. She thought you would be safe with me. She believed he'd given up. He wants to take you back to the underworld and marry you. He wants you to be the new queen of the underworld."

"But I'm his daughter!"

"Exactly," Rooster chimed in. "You're considered a demi-god and he wants to create a new generation of gods who are under his command. He wants to take over Olympus and replace the gods who are there now with his offspring, which is why he needs you. He's been trying to breed the human out of his offspring to bring them closer to godhood. Your mother is also his daughter."

I looked at Yia Yia in horror. "My mom? She's a demi-god too?"

"I adopted your mother after her real mother was kidnapped. She was never found, but I suspect Hades took her. He must have realized later that she was still too human and disposed of her. I came to know all this when Lucas came to Earth. Knowing I was your grandmother, he informed me of everything that could happen. I didn't believe it at first either, but seeing his true form and his extensive knowledge about your godlike traits, like your threshold for pain, I had to trust him."

"So, my blood grandmother was a demi-god. Oh my god, I think I'm going to be sick. He's been trying to breed a female version of himself. How many times has he done this?"

Yia Yia couldn't look at me. She seemed embarrassed, as if this was somehow her fault. She just stared at the ground awkwardly.

"Thirteen," Rooster sighed. "He's bred with your family twelve times, making you 99.99% him."

My head spun, my stomach tightened, and I couldn't breathe. He had bred an almost complete copy of himself, and I was it. "But wait," I thought, "Persephone was Hades' wife. What about her?"

"I know what you're thinking," Rooster said with a piercing stare, "but she's gone. Persephone had an affair with Zeus twice and bore his two children. When Hades found out he lost his ever-living shit and banished her to the depths of Tartarus. That was four hundred years ago."

"OK … What does this have to do with Sythera and the other girls?" I asked, dreading the answer.

"Sythera," said Rooster, "is actually Aphrodite, and Marcus is actually Ares. Hades asked them to bring you to him because he can't come to Earth himself anymore. Zeus found out about his plan after your mother had you, so he forbade Hades from coming back to Earth. Earth counts as Zeus's domain. Zeus does make the rules and Hades, as well as all the gods, follow them. Hades thought he had found a loophole with his breeding plan, and he had, but that's been shut down. Aphrodite and Ares do what they want as the kind of rebel siblings, and so they adopted human bodies and have been masquerading as high school students to earn your trust and lure you to him. The other girls are the Furies from the underworld. They are supposed to help open the portal and deliver you to Hades if you refuse to go willingly."

I started to shake. Then I remembered my drawing. I ran to my sketchbook and took it out. Had I subconsciously drawn it knowing that Sythera was Aphrodite? How did I not see that?

"Ivy," Rooster continued, "Zeus enlisted Apollo, Artemis and Dionysus to stop Aphrodite and Ares from completing their mission, to protect you and stop you from fulfilling Hades' plan, and to prevent all-out war. They wanted to keep you in the dark as long as possible so you wouldn't be tempted to meet your real father. They wanted you to keep your human element and not fall into his trap of keeping his breeding plan going and making a near-one-hundred-percent copy of himself with you. You still are unaware of your "power" and still young enough that he can somewhat mould you into what he wants. If you were in the underworld, it wouldn't matter what Zeus says because that isn't his domain."

No! Nope, this wasn't happening. I hit my head when I fainted after Lucas's crash and this was all an illusion. I was delirious. I needed some proof.

"Show me your true form," I said to Rooster. "Show me what you really look like … as Hermes."

Rooster sighed and shook his head.

Suddenly he was engulfed in a blinding light. I squinted through the brightness and could just make out Rooster, or rather, Hermes, in a helmet with wings, a sheer white toga that hung above his knees, gladiator sandals also with wings and brilliant golden skin that shone. I shook my head and slapped myself in the face to make sure I wasn't seeing things. I quickly looked at Yia Yia. She was smiling. She knew. This was all true!

In a booming voice that I didn't recognize he said, "Believe me now?"

I nodded furiously, covering my ears.

He returned to his human disguise and smiled.

I was still in shock and blinded. I believed him. How else could I explain what had just happened. Maybe I was seeing things, but I found myself wanting to know more. If this was a dream or something, it was still interesting. And I honestly felt for the first time in my life that I was truly special.

"What about Apollo and Artemis? I asked. "Where the hell have they been? I've been friends with people who were trying to kill me for almost a month now. Did they not think to intervene sooner?'

"What are you talking about? You've met them," Rooster said, rolling his eyes.

"I have? Wait, is Lucas—"

"Yes, Lucas is Apollo and Luna is Artemis," Yia Yia said.

"Is Knox, Dionysus?" I asked.

"No!" Rooster said, exasperated.

"Bro is Dionysus, but he kinda got caught up in the life Sythera and Marcus made up for themselves, so he joined them and totally forgot why he was even here. He's back on Olympus now, so it doesn't matter in the slightest."

I was stunned. This was happening. I felt faint, as if I was going to pass out from sheer panic. "Wait a second," I said, "so if you're Hermes, what's your role in all this?"

He smiled. "I told Zeus about Hades' plan. I go to the underworld all the time."

"Oh, my gods. Lucas really was trying to protect me. He said I was in danger, but I wouldn't listen. But now what do I do? He's in a coma and can't keep me safe."

"I'm stepping in for my brother until he snaps out of this," Rooster said. "I may not be stronger, but I'm smarter and I'll keep you updated as best as I can. That's really all I can do for now."

"You seem overly calm about this!" I yelled at him.

"Continuous generational incest doesn't even crack the top ten of the weird shit I've seen. I once watched someone turn into a tree," he said nonchalantly.

"OK … OK, OK, OK, OK … OK," I rambled, walking out of the room. I wasn't really sure where I was expecting to go, but I was not thinking straight.

"She took that really well," I heard Rooster said to Yia Yia before everything went black again.

CHAPTER 23

Wednesday, June 30

I woke up and checked my phone. What!? . . . I had been passed out for eleven hours. It was seven thirty in the morning, but there was no way I could deal with school after what I just learned. I sat up in bed and immediately a wall of dizziness smacked me square in the face. I fell back to the pillow, groaning loudly with pain.

"Ivy?" Yia Yia said, knocking as she cracked my door open.

"Mmmhmm," I mumbled.

"Do you remember what happened yesterday?" she asked, coming over to sit on my bed.

Shade jumped up and nudged my head with concern. She curled up next to me, seemingly to keep me safe.

"Yes . . . I do," I said. My response was more delayed than I intended. "But I'm not sure I believe it all. This seems like a complete nightmare that I'm stuck in."

"Ivy, you had to know you were special before now. I knew it the moment you were born. Your mother was the same. You can't tell me you never wondered why you never seem to get hurt or feel very little to no pain when something traumatic happens. What about when your mom's boyfriend's stove exploded? You weren't standing too far from that when it happened. Her boyfriend was killed, but there wasn't a scratch on you or your mother. Another time Sharron and you were driving to your next destination and your mother fell asleep at the wheel. You were too young to remember, but she flipped over a guard rail and rolled down an embankment. Again, you both walked away with no injuries. Also, I don't know how many physical fights you have been in but in any struggle against a mortal you would win. Against a god, you still have an incredibly good chance to be victorious. This has been going on your whole life. I don't think you realize how many times you have actually cheated death. This all has to account for something.

"Please Ivy, I know it sounds ridiculous but you must believe us. I know you know I'm not crazy and I don't play sick jokes, so the only other explanation is that I'm being truthful. And, if that's not enough, you saw Hermes in his true form!

"Ivy, I really wish I didn't have to put you in this position, but it's what's best for now. ... If you cut off your contact or end your friendship with those girls now, they will know right away, and we need all the time we can get ... until Lucas pulls through or until I figure out how to get you somewhere safe."

I shook my head. Everything Yia Yia was saying made sense. It was all there in my history. I was just too wrapped up in my hatred for Sharron, and in feeling unloved, I never noticed how lucky I truly was. It wasn't really luck though; it was real immortality. I still couldn't believe it, but if I fought this evidence, I would drive myself crazy. This wasn't just going to go away. I stared at Yia Yia and willed her to tell me it was all fake. But the moment never came.

"Wait. If gods can't get hurt, then why is Lucas lying in a hospital in a coma right now?" I asked, trying to poke holes in her story.

"The body that he is in is just a vessel. Same goes for Rooster, Luna, Sythera, Marcus and all the Furies. But his vessel was so damaged in the crash that it's almost like he's trapped inside. He's in a limbo sort of place I suppose trying to fight his way back. But there's no telling how long that will take."

"I'm still skeptical, Yia Yia, but you have no reason to lie, so I guess I'm ready to hear your plan on how this should be handled," I said with my eyes closed. I couldn't look at her and not think I was going to see her crack a smile and say it was all a joke at any minute. I wished she would.

"The next step is to act like nothing is out of the ordinary. You have to keep going to school like nothing has changed but don't go anywhere alone with them, especially that Sythera girl," Yia Yia explained. "I talked this over with Rooster and he will keep an eye on you, but we are on our own until Lucas wakes up or until Zeus sends someone else, which according to Rooster isn't likely because they are already too involved. Zeus doesn't want to create worldwide panic."

"I'm scared. Now that I know who and what they are how can I act like there's nothing wrong? How far do I have to go with this?" I asked, shivering.

"You're going have to try and do your best. Play dumb. I know this is asking a lot and potentially putting you at risk, but I promise I will not let them take you," she said, wrapping her arms around me. "Until Lucas wakes up or more help is sent, somehow you need to keep those girls in the dark. You need to make them think you trust them and that you will go with them willingly. I'm trying to get a hold of some friends who will take you and keep you hidden."

"I don't know if I can do this, Yia Yia. I'm not leaving you. I'm not particularly good at lying. My emotions sometimes get the better of me, and what if I slip up? This is all way too much for one person to handle," I cried, burying my face in my hands.

"Get out of your own head. I know you can do this. Just act normal. Rooster will be nearby even if you can't see him," Yia Yia assured me. "You'll be OK."

I had no other option. This wasn't up for debate. It just had to happen whether I wanted it to or not. The only question was could I actually fool them into thinking I didn't know.

"OK, I'll do it." I agreed. "But Rooster better be on his game. I doubt I could fight them off if I had to."

"I don't know about that, Ivy. You are 99.99% god. You have to have some kind of god-like strength. Maybe you just need to learn how to access it."

She was right. My inability to feel much pain could come in handy, and I was sure I would be able to use my godlike talents if I could learn how before Sythera and the girls decided to carry out their plan. This was no longer just a betrayal; it was war. I wasn't going to make it easy on them. Afterall, I was fighting for my life.

CHAPTER

24

Thursday, July 1

The next morning, I texted Nova to tell her what had happened to Lucas, though she probably already knew. I asked her for a ride to school and explained that I was away the day before because Yia Yia was really upset about Lucas.

Nova showed up a few minutes later and we were off to school. I was still reeling from what I had learned, and I didn't know what to say to her anymore. I kept looking everywhere else but at her and tried to focus on keeping my breathing normal.

"Why are you so quiet?" Nova finally asked.

"Just what happened to Lucas was so crazy. I'm still a little stunned," I scrambled, finding it surprisingly easy to come up with a believable lie given the circumstances.

"If you ask me, he deserved it. He really is a horrible . . . person," she spat.

"You should talk," I thought.

"Hey, why aren't you wearing the necklace we bought you?" she asked, seemly offended.

I couldn't think of a sufficient lie. I started to panic. "I . . . didn't want it to . . . get broken."

"Broken?" Nova asked. I could tell she didn't believe me.

"Yeah, you know like get ripped off accidentally or get caught on something," I explained.

"OK . . .?" I could tell she was suspicious, but I was hoping she would just let it go. I was going to throw that thing in the garbage disposal when I got home later.

The first half of the day went by in a blur, as had most of the whole week. I just tried to act normal like Yia Yia had said.

The worry and uncertainty Sythera and the girls had been showing seemed to have been totally forgotten about and their charade was back to its original perfection. They had all heard about Lucas and, not surprisingly, they all felt the same way Nova did.

"So, what should we do this weekend?" Nikki asked as Nova and I sat down with them at lunchtime. "School is over Friday, so we should celebrate."

"Ice skating?" offered Jill.

Sythera shut it down.

"Tanning?" Nikki suggested.

"I don't need it," Sythera sang, flipping her hair. "Though my nails could use some work. We will get mani-pedis this weekend."

"Great! Nova, Ivy you in?" Jill asked.

Nova nodded, but I couldn't decide if a nail salon was too secluded or not.

"I have to ask Yia Yia," I answered.

"What? You have never had to before," Sythera pointed out.

"Well since all the stuff with Lucas—"

"STOP MENTIONING THAT PRICK AROUND ME!" Sythera screamed in an unearthly fashion. The sheer force of her words made it feel like my ears would bleed.

I shook off the fear as quickly as I could and apologized. I didn't push it further. "I'll run it by her. I'm sure it will be fine."

When Rooster drove me home after school, I told Yia Yia about the plan to go to the nail salon. She said that was fine and that Rooster would be close by in case something happened. I texted Nova that I'd meet them there.

Friday, July 2

After school that Friday, the last day of school for the year, I made my way to the Glitter Gals nail salon and texted Rooster. I didn't see him, but he assured me that I was in full view as were Nova and the other girls.

"Ivy! Over here," Nova called, waving me over to the waiting room. "I am so happy we are finally done school. Next year will be great. We are just picking our nail polish colours," she said, handing me a board lined with fake nails of every colour you could think of. I picked a sparkly turquoise and sat down feeling claustrophobic. Were they just biding their time? Did they really not know I was onto them? I had a feeling they knew I knew. It was all very confusing, and I felt myself becoming increasingly paranoid. I just prayed I could keep it together.

As we all sat down in big lavish white armchairs and let our feet dangle in the soothing footbaths, Sythera started to fill everyone in about the rest of our weekend plans. Now that I knew she was Aphrodite, I finally understood why the girls did whatever she said. I felt a little rebellious now that I knew but I knew it would be too suspicious if I objected to her plans now.

"I thought tomorrow we would go to the beach," Sythera declared.

Everyone including me agreed like good little minions.

"We can spend most of the day there then head to town and have dinner," Sythera said.

Again, everyone agreed. Then she invited us to spend the night at her house afterwards.

I had to draw the line there. I couldn't be alone with them all night. Since Yia Yia had previously said I couldn't spend the night anywhere until she could trust me again, I didn't have to lie. I filled the girls in about my punishment for drinking underage, and they all seemed disappointed.

"Sorry, but if you ever want me to sleep over again, I have to obey what my grandmother says," I explained.

"How are you even supposed to prove you're trustworthy?" Jill asked.

I shrugged. That was a good question, but I really didn't know how to answer that.

"She probably means, earn it back," Nova offered. "Like follow all the rules until she decides you've learned your lesson?"

"Damn. I am SO glad I live with . . . well, Trevor . . . this week," Nikki mused.

Sythera nodded.

It occurred to me then that they probably didn't have parents. I assumed none of them did. Though I was really into Greek mythology, I didn't remember there being much information on the Furies.

The nail techs started to poke and scrape at my nail beds pushing back my cuticles.

"Oh, my goodness, I'm so sorry!" the manicurist said.

"For what?" I asked.

She looked down at my hand.

I held up my hand to examine it and she had cut into my cuticle.

To most people, this would hurt or be uncomfortable, but I hardly felt it. I had always had a high pain threshold but never thought about it as something inhuman. I rarely got hurt as a kid. I was invincible when it came to things that have should have bruised me at least. Headaches had always plagued me, but I had never really been seriously hurt, even in that gas stove explosion when I was a toddler. Now I began to wonder if all my childhood accidents had really been accidents or if we just had bad luck. Most of the places we seemed to have lived in had faulty appliances that never worked or caught on fire a lot or the water was never hot or came out brown and smelling like sweaty socks and that always resulted in us moving again.

Maybe Sharron wasn't to blame after all. Maybe she really was just trying to keep me safe. Maybe she was so distant and didn't want to become attached in case she couldn't protect me. In case she lost me.

Thinking about my mother made me miss her for the first time . . . ever. I wished I could tell her I forgave her for moving us about and that I now understood why. She still hadn't texted Yia Yia or me her new number so I guessed it would have to wait. It also made me worry about her. She was pretty scatterbrained, so I was hoping she just forgot. I could never really know until she called, but I just prayed she was OK.

CHAPTER

SATURDAY, JULY 3

The next day at the beach the girls were dressed in all-new bathing suits ... except Jill. She looked like hell. She looked tired, as if all her energy had been zapped. She was actually resting, almost like she was sleeping. I wasn't actually sure if any of them even did sleep. The morning after the party could have been a front. They probably weren't actually asleep and unaware.

"Jill? Are you OK?" Nova asked.

Jill silently nodded.

"Sit up, Jill!" Sythera roared. "You're useless if you keep moping over Bro. He's gone! Get over it!"

Jill sat up and shuttered at Sythera's words.

"Take it easy, Sythera," Nova said, "Can't you see Jill is really having a hard time? What if Marcus left you? Wouldn't you be heartbroken?"

"That would never happen!!" Sythera shot back.

There was no doubt Sythera was getting impatient with being mortal and the charade's appeal was wearing off for her.

"Oh, look who it is!" a sickly-sweet voice floated over. "Queen bitch and all her little skanky friends."

It was Joy, bouncing along the beach with her friends Brandy and Brittany trailing behind her, their blonde hair tied up in perfect ponytails and designer shades perched on their fake noses.

"Go away, Joy! We aren't in the mood for your bullshit today," Sythera growled.

"Oh, I'm so sorry your highness. I didn't know this was a sluts-only meeting," Joy laughed.

"I'm warning you!" Nikki seethed as she stood up.

"Oooh, I'm soooo scared," Joy snickered. Her mocking act cleared, and she got a devilish look in her eye. "Sit down. You're pathetic!" Joy sneered. She then smiled and kicked sand at Nikki, hitting Sythera in the face.

Joy started to laugh and all at once I saw her get knocked to the ground by a black blur. It was so fast it took me a few seconds to realize it was Jill. She was on top of Joy pinning her arms back with her knees and punching her in the face relentlessly.

People started to gather around.

"Stop it! Stop it!" Brandy screamed, rushing to help Joy. She jumped on Jill's back, but Jill wouldn't stop. Jill threw back a fist and knocked out Brandy. Brittany didn't dare challenge Jill and watched in horror as her friend tried to claw and block Jill's blows. Kicking her legs and screaming in pain, Joy pleaded for help. No one wanted to challenge Jill, but someone had to stop her before she killed Joy.

The other girls just watched from their towels. Sythera was busy brushing sand off herself and the other girls were smiling.

"Jill, stop!" I shouted.

She ignored me.

"I said, stop it!" I screamed again, grabbing one of her arms. She stood up and shoved me so hard I fell backwards.

"That's enough!" Sythera boomed.

Then Jill stopped.

She stood up as Sythera marched toward her, her feet pounding against the sand.

"How dare you!" Sythera shrieked, slapping Jill in the face hard enough that Jill's head whipped sideways and she yelped in pain.

"Ivy is our friend, and you don't hurt friends!" she raged, grabbing Jill by the neck. "Now, get lost!" she said, throwing Jill aside as if she was weightless.

Jill grabbed her towel and ran away like a scared little rat.

Nova came over to me and helped me up off the ground. "Are you OK?" she asked, concerned.

I nodded. She hadn't hurt me. I was startled more than anything.

"It's time to go. I bet the cops will be here any minute," Nikki cautioned, looking at Brittany who was crying into her phone.

We grabbed all our belongings, and I hitched a ride with Nova.

"You tried to stop this, so you have nothing to worry about," Nova assured me as we drove. "Sythera will take care of everything. Jill has gotten us into trouble before. Bro curbed her rage but now that he's gone, she has gone back to her old ways. Sythera is getting really fed up with her," Nova explained, shaking her head.

We collectively decided that we would skip the dinner and sleepover that night and just lay low for a bit.

When I got home, I called Rooster immediately and a few minutes later he was there.

"Did you see what went on at the beach?" I asked him as he sat on the couch in the den.

"Yeah," he said looking down.

"Why the hell didn't you do anything! You could have stopped her or gotten Luna!" I scolded him.

"I can't take on three Furies and a goddess and win; also, Luna still hasn't left the hospital and won't any time soon," Rooster said, trying to defend himself. "I can't interfere with the seemly harmless matters of mortals."

"Harmless! You saw what the bitch Jill did to Joy. I would hardly call that harmless. She will have to be hospitalized," I cried.

"I'm sorry, but I can't interfere. I'm here to gather info and report back to Zeus. That's it!" Rooster said, standing up. "I have to go. I'll check in on Lucas and let you know his condition tomorrow. Don't go anywhere alone with them until I get back," he warned.

I knew better than that.

The rest of the night I turned off my phone and watched a movie with Yia Yia and Shade.

CHAPTER 26

SUNDAY, JULY 4

The next morning, I woke up to a million texts from Nova telling me everything was OK, and that Jill wanted to take us all out to lunch to apologize. Rooster hadn't gotten back to me yet and I certainly wasn't going to go anywhere with them without him close by. I texted him to see if he was on his way back.

Rooster: Go ahead. Keep up appearances. Be there as soon as I can.

I borrowed Yia Yia's car and met the girls at the Bean.

As I walked in, I saw all the girls crowded around a table near the dessert bar.

"Ivy, I'm so glad you could join us," Sythera said, getting up to hug me. I tried not to stiffen when she folded me into her arms, but I thought she felt it.

"I understand. Still shaken up from yesterday?" she said, patting my shoulder.

I just smiled and nodded as I sat down.

"I'm sorry, Ivy," Jill said as she pushed a smoothie toward me. "I don't know what came over me."

"You were teaching that whore a lesson. She should have kept walking," Nikki cackled.

"Now, now girls, that's no way to talk. Jill went too far, and she apologized, so let's leave it at that," Sythera crooned.

We all nodded.

"Let's get on with our lives and decide what we should do for the next few days," Nova suggested.

"Well, I have a couple of prior engagements this week," Sythera mused, "but I can do something on the weekend."

I could tell she was planning something. Maybe I could let Rooster know what she had said, and he could follow her … if he wasn't already listening. I tried to look nonchalant by just sipping on my smoothie and listening silently.

After we had all finished, Nova took me back home and Rooster showed up soon after. I told Yia Yia and Rooster all about what Sythera had said. Rooster had a suspicion about what that meant and said he would keep an eye on it and for me to lay low for a few more days.

As per Rooster's instructions, I spent the evenings that week watching movies with Yia Yia and Shade and making meals for Luna. Being a goddess, we knew she didn't need to eat to sustain herself; she only ate for the sheer taste of it, so we made her richly flavoured food and packaged it up. Once Rooster's investigation was done, I would take it to the hospital for her.

I dodged every opportunity Sythera and the girls gave me to hang out, whether it was hanging out at Sythera's house, going shopping, out for coffee, or even going for a hike. I was getting rather good at thinking up reasonable lies about why I couldn't make it.

Monday, July 5

The next week I finally broke down when Nova asked me to go for a drive with her. We drove out to her dream farm. The sun was setting, and I followed her to a tree swing at the edge of the property.

"I wish I could just quit school completely and marry Jason and start my new life," Nova said, swinging back and forth carelessly.

Did she really think she had a future with Jason, a human, after they dragged me to hell? Was that why they were doing this? Did Hades have the power to resurrect them? Give them another chance at life?

I wanted to ask her why she insisted on listening to Sythera and being her puppet. Nova had to have a mind of her own. Every living creature does. Maybe that didn't include Furies and she didn't have a choice, but her delusion broke my heart. Nova wasn't like the others. She felt there was more to life than just serving Sythera. She had it all planned out, and I found myself feeling sorry for someone who was ultimately trying to kill me. If she was going to condemn me to a life of servitude to a demon in hell so she could have a relatively normal life on Earth, why didn't I hate her? Was I losing sight of reality?

"It will happen for you, Nova," I assured her with more empathy in my voice than I felt, "one day."

Maybe secretly I was hoping she would get what she wanted, but I also wanted to be a part of it … to visit her someday with my kids and grow as friends.

The bitter taste of a future that could never happen made my stomach ache. We stayed at the farm until the sun went down then started back home.

As we were driving, we saw a car parked in a little square that was cut out of a cornfield just off the main road. The windows were all fogged, and the car was rocking back and forth. The obvious signs made Nova and I giggle until Nova slammed on the breaks.

"What's wrong?" I asked, alarmed.

Her eyes were wide like she had just released something. She threw her truck in reverse and sped all the way back to the steamy car.

"Nova, what are you doing?!" I said, holding on for dear life.

"That's Jason's car!"

Skidding to a stop, she flew out of the truck in a rage. She ripped open the rear door of Jason's car, pulled out a fully naked girl and threw her into the cornfield behind her. Then I saw Nova climb into the car and start screaming and hitting an equally naked Jason. I jumped out of Nova's vehicle just as the girl stood up trying to collect her clothes. Then I noticed who it was.

"Nikki?!"

She looked rattled by the force of the throw, but she was aware of what she had done.

"Nova, stop!" I heard Jason yell from the car.

Ignoring Nikki, I used all my strength to pull Nova off Jason and get her back to the truck.

"I'll kill you, you evil little skank!" Nova screamed at Nikki. Nikki just got dressed and took off into the cornfield.

I could see Jason pulling on his pants. He seemed completely unaware of what was going on or why he was naked.

I got Nova into the truck and as I got in, she threw the truck into drive and plowed right into Jason's car. Luckily, he was standing off to the side by then. I saw him fall to his knees and run his hands down the sides of his face in horror as she pulled back from the mangled bumper and drove off.

We stopped at a crossroads not too far down the road when Nova spotted Nikki come barrelling out of the field. When Nikki saw us, a look of terror took came over her face just as Nova revved the engine. Nikki took off running with Nova right on her heels, trying to run her down. Nova laughed like a psychopath in a thriller movie and tried to bump Nikki so she would fall.

"Nova, stop! Please stop!" I begged her.

Even if Nikki was a Fury, I didn't want to see anyone run over.

Nova slowed down and let Nikki get away. As we watched her run, I realized it was Nikki's silhouette I had been seeing ... running into the woods, in my window, in the parking lot, at Chloe's house ... and the one that made Lucas swerve off the road.

I felt my face get hot and now I wished Nova had killed her. Nova stopped and rested her head on the steering wheel.

"How is this going to change their group dynamic?" I wondered. "There's no way Nikki can just apologize, and everything will be fine this time."

I wasn't sure what to say to Nova. What could I say? I knew better than anyone what it felt like to be betrayed and nothing anyone said would make it hurt any less. It did look like Jason didn't know what happened until Nikki was thrown off him, but it still was hard to see. Against my better judgement, I ignored the plan and gave into my feelings. I wrapped her up in a hug of pure empathy. My heart broke for her again and even though she struggled against me, she soon gave in and broke down.

"I'm so stupid! Why did I ever think I could have a normal life," she cried.

"It's not your fault, Nova. I don't know why Nikki and Jason did that, but it's not because of anything you did. You treated them both with respect and kindness and none of this makes sense."

She sobbed harder. She knew I was right.

We just sat and I let her cry on my shoulder until she lifted her head and wiped her eyes. "I'll take you home. I think I need to be alone anyway," she said barely above a whisper.

We drove in silence back to Yia Yia's.

I told Nova to call me the next day and without answering she drove off.

"What the hell!" Rooster yelled as I came through the door. "I saw everything that happened! What the hell were you thinking?"

"What happened?" Yia Yia said, coming into the entryway. "Are you OK?"

"Yes, yes, I'm fine."

"Why the hell would you hug her like that?" Rooster interrupted. "She's one of the evil demons trying to drag you to hell, or did you forget that?!"

"Yes, Rooster, I know! I'm sorry, OK. I let my feelings get the best of me."

"You let one of the Furies hug you?!" Yia Yia asked, horrified. "How could you let your guard down like that?"

"I'm really sorry. It will never happen again," I tried assuring them.

"Damn right it won't!" Rooster shouted. He stormed out the door and was gone.

"I need to do something, Yia Yia. I'll be in my room," I said, just realizing I needed to finish reading Chloe's journal while I still had a chance. I had a bad feeling I knew who she had been stalking.

Day 18

I went back to the house to check the basement. I figured it was crawling with sinister evidence that these bitches were monsters but there was a double-locked door at the bottom of the stairs, so I need to find another way in.

Day 19

I think they suspect me. They all kept staring at me at school today and every time

I turned around one of them was there. I don't think I'll ever find out what's in that basement with them watching me like a hawk now.

Day 21

I heard them talking about meeting in the woods near Blackwater Creek. I'm going to follow them at a safe distance and try to catch them in their true form. I think I know who they are! Sythera is obviously the leader. I need to gather more information about the other three but I'm fairly sure they are demons of some sort.

Oh my gods, Chloe was following Nova, Sythera, Nikki and Jill. She had found out what they were. They must have killed her. All this time I had been friends with Chloe's murderers! I had even felt sorry for one of them. I couldn't believe what I was reading. I shut the journal, feeling rage creep up inside me. They killed my best friend and put someone I loved in the hospital. I couldn't let them get away with this. I couldn't pretend anymore.

CHAPTER

27

Wednesday, July 7

Only one day passed before Nova returned to my house. Yia Yia had gone out to buy some groceries, and I sensed Nova was somehow aware of that.

"Oh, hi, Nova," I said, answering the door. I acted like I totally didn't expect this day to come.

Rooster backed away behind the door, out of sight.

"We need to talk," she said sternly, walking past me into the entryway.

She hadn't seen Rooster, who was now no doubt hiding and listening.

"What about?" That sounded fake even to me.

"Ivy, why are you making every excuse not to be around us? Sythera is pissed, and frankly, I'm getting tired of it too. I need you."

I started to feel that sympathy creep in again, but then I remembered they had killed Chloe. I couldn't hold back my dislike for Sythera and the rest of them any longer. "I don't care how Sythera feels!" I yelled. "Do you seriously not remember what happened? Nikki and Jason banging in his car? Ring any bells?" I screamed. How the hell could she be worried about Sythera after what happened.

Nova looked shocked.

"Sythera's a tyrant," I said, "but she doesn't scare me. I don't answer to her like you and everyone else seem to! Continue to treat her like royalty if you want, but I've had enough! You could still have a chance for the life you want. Maybe not with Jason, but he's not the only man in the world. How are you even able to look at Nikki now?!"

Nova's face matched my inner fear. I couldn't believe how bold I had become since finding out what they were. Nova swallowed hard. "You have no idea who you're dealing with. Nikki is like a sister to me, and Jason clearly didn't care about me. Nikki proved that to me. That's the only reason she did what she did. You don't know me at all if you think I would pick a man over someone who is like family to me. I never needed Jason."

"Oh, my gods Nova, do you hear yourself!? How can you say that! You're completely insane if you think Nikki did anything for your benefit. You had an entire future planned out with him. What happened to that? She wanted to break you and Jason up so you could turn all your attention back to Sythera."

"Ivy, if you can't see and commit to our friendship and how important it is then I guess we aren't as good of friends as I thought."

"I guess we never were! If I have to kiss Sythera's ass to be friends, then I'm done. I'm not going to treat her like a queen! She may be a good friend to you and the other girls, but if you have to sacrifice your morals and opinions just to earn her respect, I'm not OK with that."

That wasn't my biggest problem with them of course, but in case they didn't know I was onto them I had to make up a reason that seemed believable.

Nova stiffened. "You're making a big mistake!" she screamed before storming off to her truck.

The second I closed the door, I sank to my knees. My whole body was shaking with adrenaline.

Rooster reappeared in front of me. "You all right?" he asked, kneeling to look me in the eye.

I nodded.

I sat for a moment until I stopped shaking, then asked, "Can you take me to the hospital? I want to see Lucas."

As I walked into Lucas's hospital room, the once gloomy aura was now filled with fresh bouquets of flowers and the curtains were open, alighting the room with a warm glow. Luna was in the same spot as the last time I had seen her except now she looked tired and dirty and just generally uncomfortable.

"Luna," Rooster said.

She turned to look but didn't have the strength to stand. Her power seemed to be fading.

"Get out," she said dryly.

I looked at the food I had brought her almost a week ago that had gone untouched. The only indication that she had anything in her system was the half-empty water glass beside her.

"I'm not leaving until you at least take a shower," Rooster said, helping Luna to stand. "You have to be ready."

She looked at him in horror then at me.

"She knows," he said slowly.

Luna's eyes widened even further, and she shot a look of pure rage at me.

"I know now what you mean about this being my fault. More than before. I just want to talk to Lucas."

Her stance faltered.

"You're too weak to be of any help, so you're going to shower and then rest, and I mean now," Rooster growled.

Luna looked at him with surprise, for his bravery I supposed, but she bit her lip and nodded.

He helped her to the bathroom, and I walked to Lucas's bedside. His bruises had faded, but he still didn't look like himself. The machines beeping were the only sounds in the room for a few minutes as I tried to think of what I wanted to say.

"Lucas, it's Ivy."

I waited.

"Well . . . I understand now why you always said you needed to protect me. Yia Yia and Rooster filled me in on who I am, and I guess I wanted to say, I'm sorry; I'm sorry for you having to be involved. I know this isn't your fight, but for what it's worth I'm grateful for your bravery and . . . even though I know who you are now . . . I still love you."

I thought I saw him smile slightly, but then Luna came back from the bathroom and broke my gaze. I looked back at him and the smile was gone.

"I think he smiled," I said, stunned.

"Sometimes people in comas can do that. They can also open their eyes, laugh or even cry," Rooster said like that was common knowledge. "I wouldn't read into it," he finished, dashing my hopes.

Luna came around the other side of the bed.

"I'll be right back," she said to Lucas, stroking his face.

"Ivy, I am going to get Luna something warm to eat, then we have to go," Rooster said as he followed Luna out.

I sat for a few minutes just looking at Lucas. I couldn't believe that this broken man was really a god; the god Apollo no less ... I was in awe. It made me wonder if he did love me or if he had only said that to stay close to me.

"I meant it," I heard someone say, but there was no one around.

"Did I just imagine that?" I wondered. "Or did . . . did he?"

I looked at Lucas again.

"It's time to go, Ivy," Rooster said suddenly. I hadn't realized it but at least twenty-five minutes had passed while I was just staring at Lucas.

I nodded and kissed Lucas's forehead.

"I'll be waiting for you when you wake up," I whispered into his ear.

As I walked past Luna, she said, "He'll be OK," but she didn't look at me.

I considered that a temporary truce.

Later that night, I sat in bed numb. I was worried for Lucas and scared for myself and Yia Yia. I couldn't figure out which feeling dominated my thoughts more. I had a feeling Nova and the others knew I was onto them and that was horrifying. I tried not to let on to them that something was wrong, but it wasn't as easy as it seemed. I found myself wondering what they really looked like, if they had human feelings and if anyone besides me and the other gods on Earth suspected they weren't "normal." Obviously, Chloe had, but she was overly observant and intelligent … and it had cost her her life.

Go to sleep Ivy, Rooster texted me.

I knew he was outside, though I didn't know exactly where and while anyone else might be uncomfortable with someone watching them sleep, I was grateful. He couldn't necessarily help it if Sythera and the others came for me, but at least I'd have a heads up, a chance to defend myself.

CHAPTER

28

Thursday, July 8

The next morning, Yia Yia woke me up sooner than usual.

"Rooster told me you had a visitor yesterday," she said, sitting down to breakfast.

I jolted. I had totally forgotten to tell her. "Yeah, Nova came by to basically terminate our friendship because I wouldn't serve Sythera," I said, shrugging it off like it didn't bother me.

It honestly did bother me. Just when I was starting to feel accepted, like I belonged and would have lifelong friends, they turned out to be monsters and not even figuratively. I wondered if anyone else had ever dealt with this in the real world.

"I know this is hard for you, Ivy, but it really is what's best, and you've been doing a wonderful job."

I smiled slightly. I knew this was for the good of everyone who wasn't pure evil at least. I started to feel lightheaded and couldn't help thinking that at any second, I could literally be dragged to hell.

"I'm sorry, Yia Yia. I think I need to go back to bed. I'm having trouble processing things this morning."

"OK, well don't sleep too long. I decided I'm taking you away from here."

"Where? What about Lucas?" I was shocked. I couldn't leave him here. He wasn't out of his coma, and I promised him I'd be there when he woke up.

"I can't tell you because certain people may be listening, but I promise Lucas will be OK and we will come back eventually," she said, taking my plate.

My head started to burn. I felt like I was going to pass out again. Yia Yia had made up her mind and obviously wasn't going to put my safety in jeopardy. I couldn't even begin to think of how to change this in my current state. I had to stay. I had to stay for Lucas.

When I got upstairs, I stripped down to a tank top and underwear. My whole body felt like it was on fire, and I was sweating. My head pounded and I soon fell into a restless sleep as I tried to ignore how terrible I felt. An hour or two later I heard a loud thud from downstairs and sat straight up.

"Yia Yia!?" I yelled. I waited a few seconds before I called out for her again. My head was still burning, and the dizziness was somehow worse. Suddenly the air pressure changed, and every sound seemed muffled. Shade bolted into my room and jumped onto my lap. She started to hiss, and all her fur was standing on end.

"Aww, poor Ivy, sick in bed?" I heard an unmistakable voice say from the hallway. It was Sythera.

I tried to get out of bed but the burning in my head and the dizziness kept me from being able to navigate my way out from under my blankets. I finally kicked them off just as Sythera and the others pushed the door open. Sythera stood at what looked like seven feet tall as did Marcus, and they had a red aura snaking out from their exposed skin. Sythera wore a white toga-like dress with a wreath of flowers woven into her hair like a halo and Marcus was outfitted in gold armour. Nova, Jill and Nikki had grown bat-like wings that were folded up in a sickly burlap colour and looked like they would be slimy to the touch. Black snake-like ropes replaced their hair and fangs jutted down from their top row of teeth. Their eyes were black and soulless.

"Let get this over with. Don't fight it," the Nikki creature sneered.

Sythera flicked her wrist, knocking Nikki to the ground without touching her.

"Shut up! I give the orders!" Sythera said, her voice shaking the windows.

Shade hissed again and swatted at Marcus.

A shock wave shot out from Marcus's fingertips, and Shade was thrown from my lap.

"No!" I screamed.

Rooster suddenly appeared and ran to close the gap between me and my doom.

"You're not going to win this, you know that," he bellowed.

"And who's going to stop us? You?" Sythera laughed.

She tipped her head and Marcus grabbed Rooster by the neck, picking him up clean off the floor.

I heard cracking as Marcus tightened his grip. Nova, Jill and Nikki all started to salivate in anticipation of Rooster's neck snapping. I tried to get up to help him, but I couldn't stand. An invisible force was holding me still.

Suddenly a blinding flash of light flooded the room and Rooster disappeared. Sythera and Marcus looked around once their vision was restored. The invisible force holding me there was gone too.

"Where the fuck is he!?" Sythera screamed.

Marcus was dumbfounded. He just stood there with a completely bewildered look on his face.

Sythera turned her attention to me, and all I could think to do was scramble backwards. As they closed in on me, I kicked out my legs in an attempt to fight them off, which of course none were fazed by. I hit the wall and suddenly the pressure changed again, and I blacked out.

CHAPTER 29

I awoke to someone dragging me across the lawn to Chloe's house next door. It was dark out and I could feel the claws of one of the Furies digging into my ankle. I struggled to grab onto something—a bush, a branch, anything to try to stop myself. There was nothing sturdy enough to keep me from sliding across the wet grass. I was shivering as I still only had a tank top and underwear on, and the headache was still wreaking havoc on my body. There was a sudden jerk, and I found myself in Chloe's kitchen being hoisted on Marcus's shoulder. He carried me downstairs. The dirt floor of the basement seemed to melt around us, and I felt the stifling heat of fire behind me. I realized my hands and feet were bound.

All I could think was that I needed to run somehow, so I used the only thing I had as a weapon. I opened my mouth as wide as I could and sank my teeth into the back of Marcus's neck. I bore down until blood dripped down his back. He let out a scream and threw me down on the floor in front of him.

"My god-like abilities must work on other gods," I thought. "If only I had known sooner, I could have figured out how to channel them. Make them work to my advantage."

"Naughty, naughty," Sythera said, kneeling beside me. "This would have been so much easier if you would have just come willingly. You'll be even easier to kill than Chloe. At least she put up a fight. Quite the little detective she was," she sang, flipping through Chloe's journal. They had obviously found it in my room.

"Go to hell, you bitch!" I squeaked. My voice was hoarse and barely audible over the rumble of the ground below us.

Sythera put her hand to her ear, mocking that she couldn't hear me and smiled.

I looked around for a way out, but the room was only lit by the ever-widening crack in the floor spitting out fire.

It was then I saw them. Nova, Jill and Nikki were all in their true form. They had fully morphed into the Furies they were, and they were hideous. Their hair was slicked back and it hung between their wings. Their skin was the same burlap colour of their wings, now spread, and I could see rips and tears throughout. They were now naked but had no defining features and their faces had completely transformed into ghastly, fanged gargoyles. I tried to tell which was Nova, but they all looked too similar now.

"Won't be long now. The portal is coming along nicely," Marcus said, taking Sythera by the hand.

"I think we can help it along," Sythera said, nodding at the Furies.

One Fury grabbed my arm and bit down letting my blood pool in its mouth and then spit it into the opening in the floor. There was another rumble and the crack opened wider.

The bite burned. It was almost like I had been injected with acid. Another Fury came to my other side and bit into my leg, repeating the same ritual. The crack widened into a gaping hole. A swirling whirlpool of flames and sparks spewed into the air.

"Do we really have to kill her?" I heard a gravelly voice ask.

"Yes! How else would Hades be able to make her stay in the underworld, you moron! She has to die. Then she will HAVE to stay there. Even if she agreed willingly, she would still have to die," I heard Sythera answer barely loud enough.

Then I saw another Fury come to kneel at my head. She bent to sniff at my neck. "Oh gods, I wish they would just kill me quickly," I thought. This had to be the worst and slowest way to die. I was basically bleeding out and now I was going to have my throat ripped out while I was still conscious.

"I'm sorry about this, Ivy," I heard the Fury hiss. I knew at that moment it was Nova.

"Nova, please don't do this," I pleaded, straining to raise my voice loud enough so that she could hear me. "What about your dream life!?"

She looked away momentarily, almost as if holding back tears, then turned back to me, any shred of sympathy now clearly gone.

I heard what sounded like bones breaking. I looked up to see her unhinging her jaw. I closed my eyes and felt a single tear escape then evaporate in the heat spreading out from the portal.

I opened my eyes and screamed. Just as I was sure this was the end, I saw a gold arrow burst through Nova's chest from behind her. She fell beside me writhing and screaming in pain. Her wings flapped furiously but to no avail. Thick black blood poured from her wound as another arrow shot her again through her arm this time. Then I saw a huge sandaled gladiator foot step on her neck.

I twisted myself to move away from the creature's grip.

"Ivy! Please help me!" she screamed in her Nova voice. "Ivy, please. I'm sorry. Please help! NOOO!"

I was luckily facing away as I heard the creature's neck bones break and crumble into pieces. Then I heard a few footsteps toward me and the ropes around my wrists and ankles were cut. I pulled the remaining rope off myself and sat up to see Luna and Rooster stabbing and shooting arrows at Jill and Nikki. Luna was dressed in a blue toga with a quiver full of silver arrows strapped to her back and a bow in her right hand. Her hair was tied up in a bun and her skin glowed a brilliant white haze. She was even more beautiful than before. Her aim was flawless as she shot each arrow with incredible grace and precision.

Luna turned to me and nodded. But she wasn't nodding at me, she was looking past me. I turned, and there was Lucas. He had completely healed and looked like he had before the accident except for the fact that now he was in full golden armour, was about seven feet tall and shone with a white aura. He stepped over me and lunged toward Marcus. Rooster ran over to me with overwhelming speed and pulled me to my feet, leading me over to the stairs.

"Stay here!" he yelled over the noise and went back to fighting Jill and Nikki. His normally dirty shoes were now replaced with golden-winged sandals and his speed was astonishing as he zipped between Jill and Nikki, slicing them with his sword as he passed by before they even knew what happened. I watched as I huddled close to the stone wall.

Lucas had knocked Marcus to the ground and was aiming at Sythera with a flaming gold arrow. He looked confident he wouldn't miss. Marcus stepped in front of her suddenly and the arrow shot through the shoulder of his armour. It was no match for the sheer force and power of Lucas's arrow. Marcus reeled back in pain and tried to grab Lucas by the throat, but Lucas grabbed his wrist and twisted it behind his back.

"I don't want to kill you, but I will if I have to, brother!" Lucas screamed to Marcus from behind. Lucas wrapped his arm around Marcus's throat, squeezing hard enough that almost every vein in his arm stuck out. With his other arm, he forced Marcus toward the portal. Marcus's neck finally snapped. The entire floor shook when he hit the ground.

Sythera, seeing her fallen lover, screamed in rage and shot forward tackling Luna to the ground. She started to rip and claw at Luna's face. Luna did her best to push her off, but Sythera used her legs to pin Luna's arms to her sides. Sythera's rage was overpowering the huntress goddess until Lucas ran to Sythera and grabbed her hair, pulling her off Luna.

At the same time, Rooster was kicking four lifeless bodies into the portal and I knew it was Jill, Nikki, Nova and Marcus. Lucas wrapped his arm around Sythera's waist, constricting her and keeping her arms pinned to either side as he walked to the portal. Then with his other hand, he grabbed the back of her neck and hung her over the edge of the opening. "Burn in hell, bitch!" he yelled and let her go.

There was a deafening scream as she fell, and I covered my ears and closed my eyes as the whirlpool swallowed her. The portal then snapped shut as all light was snuffed out.

CHAPTER 30

Thursday, July 22 (two weeks later)

Lucas and I sat on my bed watching the rain fall in big fat drops drenching everything it touched. Yia Yia had been in the hospital for almost two weeks recovering. She had suffered a concussion and a few broken bones from her efforts to stop Sythera and the others from getting to me. I recovered more quickly from my limited injuries, which were just a few bites and bruises. I had lost a lot of blood, but it was replenished rapidly. Perks of being a goddess, I supposed. Shade had also survived and only suffered a fractured rib. Sharron was OK. She had called not long after we got home from the hospital, and she was safe.

"Zeus has decided to banish Aphrodite and Ares from Olympus," Lucas explained.

Lucas had made it back to his human vessel, so it was a lot easier for me to focus on his words and not his looks.

"I don't know if it will last," he continued, "because Zeus tends to have a soft spot for his siblings at times and may allow them back. We can only hope he won't. They were never supposed to kill anyone but you, and somehow, they convinced Hades that they had to kill Chloe to keep the plan in motion. Hades wasn't a part of the decision to kill Chloe, but he still let it happen. Zeus is trying to figure out how to stop this from happening again," he continued.

"Well, I hope there is some way he can stop Hades from torturing my family any longer and keep me out of the underworld," I said, fearing the worst.

"The punishment will be swift, but I can't promise you anything. I swear to you if there is even a chance you're in danger, I'll come back," Lucas said, touching my cheek.

"Wait, what!? You're leaving?" I said, swatting his hand away.

"I have to. I'm a god; I have a job to do. I've been on Earth too long already," he said with sadness in his voice. "I wish I could stay here with you because I love you, but I just can't."

I started to cry. We had been through so much. I couldn't just let him leave.

"I will always watch over you," he said, attempting to stroke my cheek. This time I let him, and that familiar warmth spread through me. Shade raised her head as I breathed in and rubbed up against Lucas's chest to steal some of the warmth as well.

Yia Yia knocked and came into my room just as Lucas got up to leave.

"Take care of yourself, Lucas, dear," she said, throwing her arms around him.

He hugged her back. "I will," he smiled. Then he bent down to me. "I love you, and I always will," he whispered in my ear. Then he met my eyes and kissed me.

"I love you too," I whispered back.

He stood and smiled as a hot white light enveloped him. I kept my eyes fixed on him until his features faded and the light blinded me. When I was able to focus again, he was gone.

They say it's better to have loved and lost than never to have loved at all. "Well, *they* have probably never loved a god," I thought.

I was very privileged to have someone like Lucas, or rather Apollo, watch over me, and no matter what happened he would always be there to protect me. I knew I would see him again. Come hell or . . .

www.ingramcontent.com/pod-product-compliance
Ingram Content Group UK Ltd.
Pitfield, Milton Keynes, MK11 3LW, UK
UKHW042001230426
12048UKWH00009B/478